The Executor

ALSO BY

MICHAEL KRÜGER

The Cello Player

Michael Krüger

The Executor

A Comedy of Letters

Translated from the German
by John Hargraves

Harcourt, Inc.
Orlando Austin New York San Diego London

www.HarcourtBooks.com

This is a translation of *Die Turiner Komödie.*

The publication of this work was supported by a grant from the Goethe Institute.

Library of Congress Cataloging-in-Publication Data
Krüger, Michael, 1943–
[Turiner Komödie. English]
The executor: a comedy of letters/Michael Krüger; translated from the German by John Hargraves.—1st ed.
p. cm.
I. Hargraves, John. II. Title.
PT2671.R736T8713 2006
833'.914—dc22 2006100935
ISBN 978-0-15-101268-8

Text set in Adobe Caslon
Designed by Linda Lockowitz

Printed in the United States of America
First edition
K J I H G F E D C B A

When I leave a city, it seems to me
it comes to an end and ceases to exist.

—Marina Tsvetaeva, *Earthly Signs*

The Executor

Chapter 1

HARD TO SAY, IN THE END, how many people were gathered in the little chapel. Fifty, maybe? In any case, the low, semicircular room was filled to the last chair. Death could barely find a place between the priest and that congregation of mourners. But it was there, in that moldy smell peculiar to all cemetery chapels and funeral halls, a smell that becomes more familiar to us as our best years pass by, but that we never quite learn to identify—mold, rot?—perhaps because we cover it with the insistent sweetness of the incense, the flowers, and the clouds of perfume exuded, on such occasions, by men and women alike. The aggressive use of scent, however, cannot keep the peculiar odor of these chambers from settling on our clothing and skin, sometimes clinging there until our own dying day. Unless our survivors insist on cremation, we are buried in this odor: this is one of the dismal facts that must run through every mourner's mind, while up front the priest and other dignitaries are doing all they can to focus attention on themselves, that is, on life. Here, there was no sense of eternal life, nor even of an afterlife.

I counted only three children, but there may have been more, hidden among the grown-ups. They were in high spirits, teasing, fooling around, and whispering loudly; obviously their presence at the burial of a stranger was unwise. A colleague of their father's, whom perhaps they had seen once—why should that elicit their respect? Their parents' ineffectual warnings, their halfhearted shushings, index fingers to lips, eyes rolling beneath raised brows, could not put a halt to the children's antics. One boy would not stop pulling the thin hair of a girl who was continually scratching her scabby arms and legs. Only after he was given a resounding slap by his victim were the children hustled outdoors, whence sounds of retribution were plainly audible, followed by the howling and blubbering of both parties. Then silence: the children had apparently made up. In a few years marriage would follow, and finally death would come for them, too. With this awful smell in their clothes. The father returned to his seat. He put his right hand to his left breast, a gesture I had never seen before in civilian life.

I was the only foreign visitor, or, at any rate, the only one obviously from Germany. And of course the only one, I told myself, who had known the deceased well. The others had lost a colleague; I had lost my only friend. And, taking a good look around the group, I was pretty sure that I was also the only one who was there not just to be seen, the only one who felt real grief. The crowd of mourners rippled and swayed as they took small steps forward and back, the better to observe their colleagues: a coral reef gently rocked by waves of discreet ambition. The men were thinking about the now vacant teaching chair, about promotion, about an increase in their prestige and salary. One man in sunglasses kept shrugging his shoulders, as if rehearsing for his new position. Neither were the women preoccupied by death or the deceased—they were too busy modeling their clothes and their coiffures. They fiddled and tweaked incessantly—even during the robotic recitation of prayers, fine hands armored with heavy rings and bracelets flashed amid the hairdos, then disappeared. Clearly, this was a group that did not often meet in plenary session, and all wanted to use the moment to best advantage.

The university president, a soberly dressed professor of constitutional law, addressed the tragic loss with heartless brevity. Then the dean of the faculty of philosophy summarized to rhetorical perfection the history of Italo-German relations, which had been promoted by the deceased in such an exemplary and selfless fashion; all through the speech he held up his left hand like the pan of a scale, and with his right heaped onto it the accumulated weight of his banalities. A fellow professor, a recent appointee who had known Rudolf only slightly, made an indifferent attempt to portray him, and failed completely. As he spoke, his gaze was fixed so unwaveringly on the back of the room that it caused many in the audience to look around. I was suddenly quite sure that I was the only person in that room who knew anything whatsoever about the man. I wanted to demolish the picture of coherence and consistency the speakers were constructing, and to give real meaning to my friend's death. But there was no consistency and no meaning. As it was, the ceremony took just under an hour; then the well-heeled party filed outside behind the priest, able at last to talk about the important things in life. No one spoke to me; I had the feeling no one even saw me. Among these mourners I alone was superfluous. In a well-organized funeral, every member has a precise function, from the deeply shocked believer to the cynical observer, and everyone knows which function to perform. I was simply standing around. I could not even play the role of the foreign guest, since I had not been identified as one.

I felt no need to linger at the cemetery, although normally one of my favorite pastimes is to invent biographies for the strange names on the graves, and Italian cemeteries in particular attract me, with the oval photographic portraits set into their stones. It is like a stroll through a giant family album: sullen, depressed-looking fathers and aunts and mothers; smart-looking cousins who crashed their motorbikes; children in their Sunday best, who died far too young, run over by cars. Face to face with the dead, it is easier to have a real conversation with them, to hear their crazy life stories, their forbidden love affairs with ladies and gentlemen now mouldering beneath sumptuous floral arrangements a few yards farther down the row, their images hesitantly conceding what their epitaphs conceal—that every marriage is a misalliance. Always the wrong woman, the wrong man, followed by fifty years of the usual bourgeois tragedy, and at the end, that strained smile—found out at last!—on an oval-shaped photograph.

It's hard to understand, in fact, why we don't observe this custom in Germany. Everyone has a face: why not show it? Why shouldn't we be able to preserve this unique creation we have worked at our entire lives on our gravestones, the last trace of ourselves we leave behind? Before the ceremony started, I had visited the open grave into which Rudolf would disappear, and taken a look at the faces of his neighbors. Both women: he would have liked that, of course. One of them was a maternal, plumpish person with a wart that looked as if it had been pasted onto the vertical furrow between her nose and her mouth: a big, dark, and magnificent wart no other woman in Turin could carry off as well. Her name was Emilia. The other, Elisabetta, had been on this earth only nineteen years. She had not even had time, I thought, to create her own face, she looked so gaunt, so colorless.

I found it impossible to imagine Rudolf inside that gold-trimmed black casket. A luxury model of the tackiest kind. A fantastic gaffe. And now Rudolf, who had always described existence itself as pointless hard labor, as a titanic effort, was being propelled effortlessly over the crunching gravel in this luxurious behemoth, this Rolls-Royce of coffins, as if it weighed nothing. All life, he had written in one of his last letters, is nothing more than a series of diminishments, limitations, concessions, annihilations, a progressive renunciation that brings us, after forty or fifty years of self-pondering, to the core that makes us what we are. Half a century to sort out false interests, false viewpoints, false opinions, from true ones. To recognize false music, false literature, false philosophers, false surroundings, and false people. Since we are glutted with things that are not good for us and avoid the things we need, it takes us this long to understand the world and ourselves. In any case, Rudolf had taken that long to know exactly what and whom he could do without. Would he still be alive if he had not been so literal about it? Now he was lying in a false coffin.

I wanted more than anything to steer clear of this false funeral party. No handshakes, no shared memories, no funeral repast, no fuss and feathers. I just wanted to get out of there.

I had made an afternoon appointment to visit Elsa at the hospital. If there was still time afterward, I could come back and bid Rudolf farewell in my own way.

Over the cemetery hung huge white clouds with dark, frayed linings. Treacherous-looking clouds. I hoped it wouldn't rain.

Chapter 2

NOT FAR FROM THE CEMETERY I found a bar with a few tables set out on the sidewalk. And wouldn't you know it, in this out-of-the-way suburb of Turin I ran up against one of those surly waiters who have plagued me my entire life. I had to signal several times before he would interrupt a life-and-death conversation with a blonde at the next table to acknowledge my request for coffee. When he reappeared, with a hefty brown cup, he resumed the conversation, allowing the cup to hover for a while above my table before setting it down with a clatter. Rudolf had always gushed about the disciplined politeness of Italian waiters, their precision and speed; he had gone so far as to write a feuilleton article—frequently reprinted—in which he sang the praises of those who ply the waiter's trade. Lucky for him he'd been spared this rude slacker, who now carelessly dropped the bill on my table; it took off from the metal surface with the first gust of wind and fluttered around the blonde's feet. She crossed her legs, showing whitish creases on her upper thighs formed by the plastic upholstery of the chair. I could not help staring at that field of striated flesh emerging from beneath her bright red faux-leather skirt. The waiter moved to the doorway and stood there, a round tray in the crook of his arm, carrying on about the African prostitutes who walked this quarter but gave the restaurant no business. "They send the money they take from the Italians home," he said. "Third-world developmental aid." It made me uncomfortable to have this man in my immediate vicinity.

Rudolf had taught in this city for more than twenty years. He'd begun his career in Rome and Naples, as a lecturer with the German Academic Exchange Service. After completing his study on Kierkegaard (a study now famous in philosophical circles), he was granted a lecturer's position in Turin. This position was later converted into a full professorship. He had always made a great mystery of this appointment, which was an unusual one. But in those days everything seemed to go his way. So much so that I was not at all surprised when, a few years later, he was asked to set up his own institute and given a palazzo to set it up in. At his disposal was a spacious penthouse apartment with a rooftop terrace, where he worked underneath once white, now dirty-gray awnings from March to October. The rent was a joke, and the view over the rooftops was priceless.

This terrace was also where Rudolf kept his zoo, which had attained a certain celebrity not only in Turin but among his friends and enemies in Germany as well, though Rudolf habitually pleaded with them all not to breathe a word of it.

He was afraid the university or the municipal authorities might forbid him his little game preserve. And they would have had good reason to do so, for the sanitary conditions obtaining at this zoo were far from acceptable.

The king of Rudolf's terrace was a good-natured, malodorous dog aptly named Caesar. As Caesar aged, his fur began to thin, until he strongly resembled a pig. Caesar was a German import, the gift of a friend from Rudolf's student days, whose father in Goslar—why, of all places?—had bred these weird-looking *Schweinshunde*, selling them for large sums all over the world. Besides the dog, Rudolf kept an assortment of ordinary chickens and a few exotic ones; several ducks of varied background, domestic and feral, and a goose, for whom a partner of appropriate social standing had been sought for years, to distract her from an ongoing affair with a widowed peacock. There were all kinds of cats and turtles, and a hedgehog that would patter by beneath its heavy burden of spines, while Rudolf pursued philosophy under one of the umbrellas. My favorite animals were his dwarf rabbits, with their elegantly patterned pelts; each had a name from Proust's *Recherche,* and, even while hopping about, they arrogantly maintained the dignity their titles conferred.

The laws of this jungle were simple. Eating one another was forbidden. The cats left the salamanders and other creeping creatures in peace, and kept their paws out of the bowl of lethargic goldfish. Killing for sport was outlawed, along with any sort of ritual sacrifice. These few rules were the main pillars of terrace social life, which must be obeyed by all. But *why* they were obeyed remained Rudolf's secret. Perhaps it was because almost all of these animals knew only this little quarter of the world, unless they knew the rest from hearsay, from avian gossips traveling through, and from sounds that penetrated upward from the bustle of the street below. Below—well, that was Hell. Don't expect anything from down there, Rudolf often said, where what humanity calls reason ensures a continuing chaos. There are no solutions where brutality and stupidity set the tone. Both were unknown on the rooftop terrace. An ideal society, Rudolf said: no conflict, no war, no bloodshed, even though no one animal understands any other. But what do we know? Nothing. Of course, the Latin spoken by tortoises sounds strange to the ears of modern-day ducks. They get along because they understand nothing of one another and therefore have to be especially considerate. If a member of this anything but homogeneous group happened to die, it was given an honorable send-off and promptly replaced, causing no strain on terrace society. Conflict, if it arose at all, came exclusively from outside, as when migrating birds landed in this paradise, boasting about their adventures and trying to steal food from the indigenous population. Status, power, respect—seeds of conflict anywhere else—caused no struggles here. Even the pigeons that sometimes mobbed the roof terrace, while not welcomed, were at least tolerated.

Rudolf was a kind of general director not only of the zoo but also of the botanic garden that surrounded it, which grew with the years into a kind of contained jungle. Elsa, along with a constantly changing cast of domestics, mostly from Thailand or Africa, who spoke no Italian, had the demanding job of general caretaker. Caesar discharged the responsibilities of deputy director. It was known as Rudolf's ark, but if anyone mentioned this word in his presence Rudolf might end the conversation right there. "No one is being saved, and certainly not on an ark," he would growl, and leave the room.

On the floor below the apartment was Rudolf's brainchild, the Institute for Communications Research, which he treated as his private fiefdom. If Elsa was to be believed, there was not much communicating happening there, let alone research. Rudolf hated holding seminars and having to read students' papers. There was nothing to be learned from students, in his opinion, except how not to dress and feed yourself.

As time went by, he also began to avoid the city that lay at his feet. He had taken a childlike delight in Turin in his first year, but after that it became routine. The more he kept away from the city, the more unapproachable it seemed. As a rule, the better we get to know a place the more we love it, but with Rudolf the exact opposite was true.

Besides, he was always traveling. When you tried to reach him on the telephone, eight times out of ten you would be told that he was at a conference abroad, and even when "abroad" was Germany it was impossible to get hold of him. If you actually got him on the other end of the line, you had to make it brief, because he had to pack. Tokyo,

Harvard, London, Lyon. Internet or no Internet, people still like seeing each other face to face, although from a scientific viewpoint there is nothing to be gained from it. "Thank God there is no grapevine among the universities," Rudolf often said. "Otherwise everyone would find out that I have been giving the same talk over and over for twenty years." He had only to change the title—and since he had a knack for titles several of his essays (mostly about "the destructive side of constructive reason") actually became popular. I have never quite understood why he was so successful in academic circles, given the obviousness of his few published scientific papers. "What we at the Institute are practicing," he used to say, "is not scientific research but personal opinion; besides, no one takes us seriously. We train journalists, who are not allowed to write what they want to write anyway, and after thirty years in the field they write only what they are allowed to write." It was Rudolf's view that it would be better not to educate young people at all—better to let them do whatever they want, since they don't want to learn in the first place; clearly they knew better, and grasped things more quickly than the educated. They arrive in the world as complete human beings, know-it-alls who roll right over their more cultivated elders. The great demagogues come out of philosophy departments, he would say.

In the last few years of his life, Rudolf had written four short novels that earned him literary prizes, honors, and a great deal of money. He was translated into every conceivable language: he even received author's copies from Korea.

Yet with every award his general frame of mind worsened and his hypochondria and pessimism bloomed. With Rudolf, the peculiar but common need to be a part of some group (and to observe its inevitable rules) had given way to a rigid individualism that acknowledged only one rule, never to endorse anything or anyone. Nothing was more repugnant to him than a gathering of authors. I once took him to a literary party. For the first time, he saw a lot of writers crowded in one place: novelists, poets, and a few old-fashioned playwrights. He got halfway through the door, then turned around and fled. And when a German academy asked me to inquire whether Rudolf might be disposed to accept its highest prize for literature, I walked around for days weighed down by this terrible secret before I finally called him. Rudolf implored me to persuade the president to drop the idea. "You'll be saving my life," he shouted into the phone with a laugh, "if you get the jury to change their verdict. You must convince them that my books are flawed." I could not get this crazy sentence out of my mind. The thought of having to come to Germany, wearing a suit, was, for him, life-threatening. The prize went to someone who was clearly very happy to get it, because he was convinced that he did not at all deserve it—erroneous, in my opinion, but in Rudolf's perilously close to the truth. The award ceremony was well attended; the acceptance speech, which was printed in the newspaper, expounded a kind of nihilistic poetics that can still be found in any anthology of this author's work. Well-formulated nonsense. The night after the award ceremony, Rudolf called me and asked if everything had gone all right. "How was my replacement?" "It was quite an event," I said, and immediately regretted this imbecilic remark. Why couldn't I tell him the truth? In reality, I had been so embarrassed by the author's talk that I was scarcely able to follow it: it had seemed to me the manifesto of a world without shame. After hanging up, I thought Rudolf's voice sounded almost hysterical, as if he thought he had barely escaped with his life. (Later, I told this story to a larger audience, which included the prizewinner himself. When I finished, another locally well-known author, who had given up writing because he had mastered it too easily, remarked that Rudolf hadn't accepted the prize because he had been hoping for a bigger one. He had gambled and lost, said the ex-writer primly; meanwhile, he who had inherited the prize sat there looking like a thief caught red-handed.)

By now the sun was so low that only the shoes on my outstretched legs caught its rays. The woman in the red faux-leather skirt was gone. How had this eye-catching splash of color managed to slip away unnoticed? I must have nodded off. I was now the only customer. Inside the dark bar they were playing a popular song, I tried to recall the German version, but it would not come to me. Across the street I noticed a school, an imposing, brooding block; the side facing me was covered with obscenities, graffiti scrawled up to shoulder height. Semiotic salad. Some obnoxiously young-looking students stood leaning against the wall smoking. They seemed content. No one paid them any attention, not the teachers intently striding toward their cars nor the old ladies in veiled hats, tripping past on spindly legs.

Strange, the sorts of people we involuntarily spend our days with. First the funeral party, then the waiter, and now these kids. Not to mention the passengers on that morning's flight to Turin: all businesspeople who had buckled their seat belts and immersed themselves immediately in the newspaper and its account of falling stock prices. A select group of masochists with carry-on luggage, who after laboring in the financial vineyards for a day will fly back in the evening. No art tourists, no pilgrims to the place where Nietzsche, in the evening of his despair, tried to save a horse that had stumbled from being whipped; no eloping lovers; no random loners—just these strange corporate travelers, without whom the airline industry wouldn't exist, business-class robots who promptly produce tiny calculators from oblong briefcases and, stony-faced, compute their stock-market losses. Not one had bothered to look out the window.

Today I'd had involuntary "contact" with a hundred people; now, sitting at my table, I wondered, how much of what society imposes on us can we put up with? How do we stand dealing with people who can't stand us? We are all geniuses at looking the other way. The man next to me on the plane had given off such an acrid smell that I'd nearly been sick. But all my attempts to change seats were thwarted by the flight attendant, and I had to cross the Alps in this unsavory company. All Rudolf had ever had to do was get out of bed in the morning, climb ten steps up to his zoo, and once a week downstairs to his seminar room, where he flagrantly ignored his students. Still—I was alive, and he was in his grave.

When suddenly a taxi appeared, I flagged it down and jumped in. Through the rear window I could see the waiter, dumbfounded, hands on hips, glaring at me for stiffing him. For the first time that day, I was the object of someone's undivided attention.

Chapter 3

THE HOSPITAL WAS AT THE other end of the city, in the hills, and the driver seemed pleased that the long ride would allow him to show me whatever points of interest Turin had to offer. A cabbie who loved his city. A city of suicides—Pavese, Levi, Lucentini, Rudolf. As in my previous visits, I felt at home right away. There are cities that force themselves on you, and others that don't show the slightest interest in you. If you don't visit them regularly, they forget about you. They fill in their construction sites to confuse you, they set up detours so you don't recognize where you are. They want more than anything in the world not to be conquered, not to be loved. But Turin, for all its evident discretion, belonged to those cities of Europe that I might have moved to, at the appropriate time, even to die. But I didn't have the good luck that Rudolf had always had, to excess, right up to his death. A lucky dog, despite his melancholia, his depressions, and his fits of violent rage. Because the city did not demand anything from him, he felt at home there.

Although from outside the hospital looked small enough to be navigable, finding Elsa's room proved to be quite a feat. Inside, hospitals are all the same, from the cheery pictures on the walls to the smell. And all of them are labyrinths that can be mastered only by doctors and nurses, not visitors. As for the patients, they know only what concerns them: their own room, the smoking lounge, and the exits. At the entrance, I was greeted by a sickly-looking delegation clad in bathrobes and fantastic bandages. Patients, displaying their stigmata: leg stumps, lopped arms, gauze-swaddled heads spewing clouds of cigarette smoke. Every new arrival capable of self-locomotion was regarded with naked hostility. Just you wait, soon enough your turn will come, they silently informed visitors, who would hang their heads in guilt.

Elsa's room was on the top floor, in a separate ward shielded by a closed glass door. What disease did you have to have to be lodged in there?

She greeted me before I was halfway through the door: "Be quiet, my neighbor is sleeping." Her whispered plea was followed by a deathly silence: no clock ticked here; the IVs that keep unassuming, hesitant Life in process dared not gurgle. And in this dry, cold, static silence only a delicate whimpering could be heard, like a timid bird. It came from Elsa's roommate, who lay flat and motionless, hooked up to an assortment of twisted tubes. She seemed to have no body. Her gray, sunken face and two strangely red hands were all that could be seen. The window was open, and as I approached Elsa's bed on tiptoe I saw two swallows swoop past with incredible speed, as if to demonstrate what a healthy body was capable of.

I couldn't think of anything to say, not even a word of comfort. Elsa gazed at me for a while with her unhealthy eyes, briefly took my hand, and squeezed it limply. I was glad when she released it, setting it down on the bed as if it were not attached to me.

"It's awful to be so defenseless," she murmured.

"When will you be released?" I asked.

"Who knows? Two or three days, a week?"

Then, since there was nothing to discuss, and every unnecessary word only exacerbated the wounds that were supposedly being healed, she took the apartment key from the nightstand drawer and gave it to me, explaining in mumbled phrases, broken by long pauses, how I was to get up to the terrace. Shakily, she scrawled the names of the two girls who looked after the animals.

"You can look through everything," she said. "I hope you will find your way through Rudolf's secrets. And take care of Caesar—he probably misses Rudolf the most."

Her voice had grown so soft and hoarse that I was relieved when a nurse came into the room and cheerfully ordered me to leave. Was I looking at a dying woman? Or were the medicines to blame? On the nightstand I'd seen a tray with many little compartments overflowing with colored pills, and when I leaned over to peer at the labels I noticed an exact timetable for administering these poisonous-looking treats. I was certain that Elsa did not ingest any of them voluntarily. On the table, there had been none of the offerings one normally finds in hospital rooms, though there had been a generous heap of them on the nightstand of her moribund roommate: fruit (mostly oranges, which can be peeled only with difficulty—if at all—by the mortally ill), cookies, chocolates, flowers, magazines, and a book. Elsa was obviously too lethargic to read, and the fact that she had not even brought one of her own books was for me the clearest indication that the night Rudolf died she must have narrowly escaped death herself. But what had happened? In the obituaries—not only the hastily composed ones that appeared in the dailies immediately after the tragedy, but also those in the lengthier weekend editions, Elsa was mentioned only as Rudolf's wife: not even the journalist from *Il Tempo,* in whose article the words *tragic* and *tragedy* played a starring role, had given a more detailed description of her. Literature had suffered a tragic loss, not the wife. The German feuilletons did not mention her name, even in *Die Zeit* and the *Frankfurter Allgemeine,* papers that had favorably reviewed her books as well as his. Did no one know how long Rudolf had been married to Elsa, or had this reticence been a mark of respect for his notorious need to isolate his private life from public view? The laconic last sentence in the *New York Times* obituary was the most detailed mention she got: "He is survived by his wife, Elsa, who also teaches at the University of Turin."

I should have asked Rudolf's colleagues at the cemetery what had happened to Elsa; my reserve had clearly been ill-advised. While I waited for the elevator in the hallway (next to an old woman under general anesthetic who had been parked there unattended), the nurse came out of Elsa's room again, but I could learn nothing from her. She would not breathe a blessed word, just gave me the malicious knowing smile of someone who was not ready to share her secret with a stranger. And if you were the patient, that smile seemed to say, I would act the same way: even in Italian hospitals, you can rely on a nurse's discretion.

A short visit. I had to force my way out through the gaggle of bathrobed patients, who were still smoking as if their lives depended on it. Out in the street I paused, a little helpless, a little superfluous, and a bit sick. I gave a coin to a beggar in a caftan who slunk by, holding his scaly hand out to passersby without looking them in the eye. He dropped the coin into his other hand without a word and quickly disappeared. A gentle rain began to fall; when it hit the hot asphalt, it released a wonderful sweet smell. I started off again, feeling a sense of relief, not caring what direction I was headed in.

At a kiosk I bought newspapers and cigarettes and a city map of Turin, then found myself a café. I circled and drew lines between the places on the map that had meaning for me: the cemetery, the hospital, the institute, and the main railroad station. The result was a sort of irregular rectangle. I needed more circles to make the city my own. I decided that I should mark in the final dwelling places of all of Turin's famous suicides. Pavese's small hotel, Primo Levi's house, which I definitely wanted to look up, Nietzsche's various addresses. I have maps, annotated in just this way, of all the cities I have ever visited. My maps have a cultic significance for me, and when I occasionally pull one out (often years later) and look at the lines I drew, they always add up to a portrait of myself in that place, a hurried but accurate sketch that sets in motion the awful comedy of memory. When I see my handwriting, though, as it used to look, I hardly recognize it—just as I have a hard time recognizing my face in old photos. I can remember places, interior furnishings, street corners, landscapes, and, in relation to them, a thousand moments: I see Rome in a thunderstorm; flecks of sunshine racing over the house fronts in the Piazza Navona; the warm scent of hay in my nostrils that reminds me of my grandfather. But in none of these pictures can I see myself. I don't appear. I don't know where I was standing, what I was thinking or saying. It should be easier for me to write Rudolf's life than my own.

The truth was, I was feeling a growing resentment toward Rudolf—quite involuntarily. Of course, I thought not of him but, rather, of Elsa, of her hot, limp hand, of her exhaustion and overwhelming grief. Rudolf had abandoned me. Because he had no talent for goodbyes, and because any sense of responsibility he might have felt for Elsa and me had been superseded by his preparations to kill himself, he had made his escape with no warning. But then empathy had never been his strong point. Sometimes months would go by before I heard from him, and then when he did call it was more an effort to clear his own conscience than a serious attempt to apologize for his silence. "I was on a steep road going to the Other Side," he would say. "Thank God I was still able to get back." But never a word about where this "other side" lay. Did you take a woman with you to this other side? He never answered such questions. On the contrary, he would immediately counter with another question: Did I really have such a naive idea of the nature of the abyss? And accompany his question with that unrestrained, malicious laughter of his, making any further questions impossible. He felt no inclination to share the secrets of his labyrinths, and when you lost your way in them he would spring out and devour your ego with sharp-toothed commentaries.

There was a swarm of gnats in the air outside the café. Rudolf, I thought, you have put me on a path that will lead me away from you. Maybe we will never meet again. And, if we do, we will no longer know each other.

Chapter 4

I HAD TO ASK MY WAY TO the *direttore*'s office. Outside the building I asked directions of the first student I ran into. She was short, with an unruly mop of red hair, barely tamed by a baseball cap, and a gleaming stud in her nose. Although she was just leaving with her bulky knapsack, she turned around and guided me to the secretary's office on the second floor, where I was received by Marta, Rudolf's colleague of the past few years. She seemed relieved to see me, though she did nothing to ameliorate her habitual sullen manner. Elsa being incapacitated, it was Marta who had called me up to let me know the date of the funeral: "If you want to come." Which I had.

Coffee, water, biscuits. The room had a vaulted ceiling painted with mythological tableaux, illuminated by a harsh white halogen light. Just another funeral parlor, except that here, on the front wall, instead of a crucifix hung a picture of Rudolf—a poster for a reading at the municipal library in Würzburg. He was smiling his bitter smile, the only one he had. Rudolf was one of those people who could not smile mischievously, or slyly, or maliciously. When he smiled at all, it was with a dry, bitter expression that transformed his face, rusty with age spots, into a landscape of wrinkles. This image hung not only in municipal libraries but also in the private chambers of many literature-mad young girls. And in Turin. Someone had clumsily tucked a rose—now drooping—between the poster and the wall. Rudolf, an expert on wildflowers, had detested roses and had categorically refused to take seriously writers who trafficked in their symbolic aura. There were two desks, one crammed with documents, notes and clutter, the other bare. On Marta's desk was a photo, its upper border torn, of her with Rudolf, next to a soda bottle containing another rose that was just about to drop its last petals. I had landed in a room where Rudolf was not understood, and that made me suspicious. On every shelf and table were copies of Rudolf's books in every possible language, from which I concluded that this branch of Rudolf's enterprise was Marta's major responsibility.

"Why did you rush off from the cemetery like that?" she asked reproachfully. "I would have introduced you to the dean, who wanted to meet you." Marta had a flat but pretty face that twitched occasionally when you were talking to her, as if reacting independently to certain words. "Rudolf" was one of those words. It darted across her features like a will-o'-the-wisp, found just the right spot, settled there, and set her skin twitching.

So I had been recognized after all as the lone foreigner. Obviously you had to be part of a horde of people to be mistaken for someone else. Anyway, my presence in the city was now known to anyone who cared to know. What the significance of this might be was unclear, but it seemed to me that it meant something. I was a player. I was someone to be reckoned with.

"I wanted to be alone," I said, and as I voiced this thought in my halting Italian, it sounded so pathetically Teutonic that I wished I could have added a little joke or some ironic remark. When someone dies, all normal people, all Italians, at any rate, like to be around other people, but of course the German prefers to deal with his pain alone. I could hardly have made a more idiotic first impression, I thought, as Marta buzzed around me like an insect. Her high heels sounded on the stone floor like the ticking of a clock. She wants to ration out my time, I couldn't help thinking. Her shoes were a dark red color.

"I can well understand that," said Marta, who had stopped directly in front of me. "As I thought of Rudolf, defenseless, penned inside his coffin, I, too, wanted to run away. He had felt hemmed in his entire life: by his background and his family, by his profession and the institute, by his marriage and especially by his writing. He was the textbook definition of a trapped person, who, with the passage of time, has finally stopped trying to escape. Giving up writing, in his opinion, was the only thing he could do to keep himself alive awhile longer. But how? If he really had to he could give up his family, his profession, and his institute. But not his background, and not his writing. At least that's what he told me," Marta concluded, and resumed her restless pacing. "His writing, that strange mix of anguish and accuracy, had to destroy him. It was only a question of time—anyone who knew him knew that. Every word he wrote was a nail in his coffin. Those who had to watch him at this carpentry day and night, as I did, were at least prepared. But you—I would not want to be in your shoes."

Was this oddly disjointed psychological profile of Rudolf nothing but Marta's own self-aggrandizing nonsense, or had she in fact seen through him more clearly than the rest of us, who had tried to believe that Rudolf's writing was his liberation from the apparently heavy burden of the rest of his life? At any rate—and here I was in complete agreement with Marta—Rudolf's body should have been cremated and his ashes scattered. But Elsa had been against it, I now learned. I had a feeling that this was not the only revelation in store for me.

There are those whose conversation at a funeral consists of the most unscrupulous and ruthless criticism of the deceased. The feeling of relief the burial engenders dissolves all inhibitions. I decided then and there that I would take no part in any such opprobrious postmortems on Rudolf.

"How long to do you intend to stay?" asked Marta. She certainly had a talent for asking questions that deserved no answers. She didn't even look at me. People who don't have much to say can make themselves seem important by interrogating others. Such people are everywhere, in pubs and parliaments, but most often in families, which as a rule are split between askers and answerers. Since Rudolf would never have dreamed of asking a question, Marta had perhaps been his ideal complement. Most askers, Rudolf had once said, already have their answer—and their questions are all rhetorical. Even so, they leap in with the answer themselves, because they are afraid that whoever they've asked might beat them to it.

Now how was I supposed to answer Marta?

"It all depends when Elsa is discharged," I said. "In any case, it's she who must decide what I should take back to Germany."

I watched Marta closely when I spoke the name of Rudolf's wife. She gazed back distantly, a bit bemused, her eyebrows raised.

"Elsa, yes." That was all she would say. To get any closer to this issue seemed risky. Marta lit a cigarette and, with the cigarette still between her lips, exhaled elaborately through mouth and nose, as if a secret were somehow codified within this clearly well-practiced routine. An oracle, but with no Pythia to interpret. All she needed to learn now was how to send smoke out her eyes and ears as well.

Although one could not accuse Marta of a tendency to overdramatize, she was an adept of the actor's cult of metamorphosis. All of a sudden there she was, sitting with her cigarette, posed like a shop clerk ready to show me her wares. And what might those be? Would she keep her position under Rudolf's successor? Since Rudolf had founded the institute, she'd probably been in on all the dirty linen, knew where he kept the stash that exists in every institute in the world. She would need to be handled with care. Most important, in the past few years, during which Rudolf's novels had come out, she had been his closest confidante, and, since the engine of international academic interest in his work was already revved up, Marta would inevitably become that engine's most important source of fuel, especially since it was uncertain when or whether Elsa would recover. And, as Rudolf's oldest living friend, I had been designated by Elsa as his literary executor. If there was one person whose trust I had to win, it was Marta. Suddenly I was sure that she knew this, that she "saw things exactly the same way." She was waiting for an offer. I had to come up with one, and fast, if I was to retain her backing. We had to form a team: one of us without the other was worth nothing.

Perhaps it was naive of me to assume that she would willingly open her vault of treasured memories and let me have a look gratis. Not until a serious offer of mutual support was on the table could negotiations on turf begin, and how long these would take was uncertain. I would have to wait, give her time. Only when she felt in control of the schedule could I start delving into the secrets of her relationship with Rudolf. But imposing this censorship on myself had led me to wide-ranging and unpleasant speculations about Rudolf's erotic life, which, leaving aside the adventures of our youth, had always appeared to honor the broad conventions of marriage rather than the uninhibited pursuit of passion. More likely, his own social awkwardness, or his growing fame, lent him an erotic magnetism of sorts, which, to a certain segment of his female readership, was more than just attraction. His shyness, his innocence of the skills of seduction (which may have been feigned) might have made a certain type of woman (a type one runs into often in literary circles) eager to snare him in a delicate net—to protect him and confine him. When Rudolf had expressed his abhorrence of social ambitions—which he liked to do, and quite crudely at that—once he had shed his armor of convention and sophistication, he made himself vulnerable and highly attractive to the kind of people who love to rescue others without in the least understanding why they suffer. He believed himself to be incurable; so sympathy, motherly affection, was the only thing that might have helped—and that was the thing that above all else he could not abide. People treated him like a star, but that, too, he found deeply repugnant. One prerequisite for monogamy, after all, is needing to be left alone by others. Men are faithful when they have no opportunity to be anything else. And then, a man who wants to be alone very often cannot bear even his own wife, and the idea of being saddled with one or more mistresses drives him to the edge of despair. After Rudolf's readings, younger women, stoically silent but smiling serenely, would wait for the line of autograph seekers to dwindle, then seize the moment. Mostly they were writers themselves, or arts-and-crafts types, people in the field, at any rate, or occasionally wealthy widows, offering their services without shame or shyness, each utterly convinced that she alone could heal this hopeless case. In the encounters I witnessed, Rudolf always deflected overtures, shyly pleading fatigue, but this very argument must sometimes have backfired: since he needed his well-earned sleep, someone would see that he got it. You don't need to say a word, a woman had whispered, after he had told her, his voice breaking, that he couldn't talk anymore, that words failed him. And then she put her hand on his arm and closed her eyes for an extended moment. I can still see the panic in Rudolf's eyes—but before the fear of getting in too deep could take effect the woman, who introduced herself as a psychologist, was invited along to a restaurant, where Rudolf found the words he thought he had lost, and the party continued long past midnight. In her spare time the psychologist wrote erotic novels dealing with tricky sexual relationships, and Rudolf asked her numerous questions. Of course, when she proposed sending him her manuscripts, the address he gave her was obviously false: Naples, via Camelia 3.

So did Rudolf have a monogamous relationship, or, perhaps, two? One with Elsa, one with Marta? I was beginning to get used to Marta's face. Her twitchiness, her general restlessness, started to grow on me; perhaps that was why I could picture her, angular and inscrutable, as Rudolf's lover. "Keep cool," I whispered to myself. "No emotions."

I needed to keep my guard up, for suddenly I, too, felt a numbing fatigue that made further thought impossible.

But, no matter how long I intended to stay, I would have to talk with the dean of faculty and the university president, said Marta, yawning widely herself. For now, however, that was her only condition for my being there. And she quickly explained why these appointments, which I would have preferred to put off, were so important to her:

Rudolf's apartment and the rooftop terrace had to be vacated by the end of the year, since a "worthy" (her word) successor to Rudolf was likely to be found by then.

As Rudolf's friend, and now his appointed executor, I would know how much time would be required to go through his literary papers. The university administration probably assumed that I would take responsibility for the zoo as well, since I was involved in clearing the place out.

"You realize, of course," Marta added, "that officially no one knows anything about the ghastly situation on the roof, and Rudolfo issued strict orders that, except for his most intimate friends, no one was to set foot in the garden, and that includes the university president. Whoever breaks this commandment will have to deal with Rudolf's curse from the grave. We shall have to find new homes for the animals and the plants. That was Rudolfo's last wish. The literature comes second. Who knows whether Elsa will ever be able to enter the house again, and, in any case, she will never be able to get through those mountains of crap."

Listening to Marta, I was beginning to get a rough idea of what awaited me.

"In the time remaining," she went on, metamorphosed from sales clerk or erotic accomplice to the host of a particularly sadistic reality show, "you have a difficult problem to solve."

She handed me a list, full of pedantic annotations, detailing personal items of Rudolfo's that were in her office: correspondence with foreign publishers and translators; manuscript copies with final corrections (which Rudolf often telephoned in); copies of translations of his works, which my polyglot friend had always corrected himself, right up to the final period, again with that self-destructive zeal that had amounted to an obsession, as if a perfect translation actually were possible; heavily corrected galley proofs; page proofs; jacket proofs done in colored pencil; and advertisements, which Rudolf always wanted to see before they were printed, because he mistrusted human beings in general, and human beings in publishing in particular. Often enough, in Rudolf's absence, I had had to appear personally at his German publisher's office to make some unbelievably petty correction to the final page proofs, which caused this otherwise pleasant person to erupt in a tirade of hate against me, the messenger, or to complain *in loco auctoris* about the advertising designs, because the color copies sent to him were not quite up to the quality he had been promised. It struck me that none of his publishers—who had all made a lot of money off their difficult protégé—had shown up at his funeral. Had I simply not recognized them? While he was alive they, in their turn, had badgered him constantly, particularly an American and a Japanese who came to Turin every year to pay their respects to the overworked and overwrought author. His German publisher—whom I certainly would have recognized—had also insisted on dropping in on him, quite often unannounced, to find out how a new manuscript was coming.

All of Rudolf's publishers had written letters of condolence to Elsa, Marta said, but Elsa hadn't wanted to see any businessmen at the funeral. No relatives or friends, either.

"And his lady friends?" I asked.

"Also no."

The door to Rudolf's office was directly behind Marta's desk.

"No one has been in there since he died," she said.

"And you?" I asked.

"I know his office by heart; I need only to walk in if I want to be alone with Rudolfo."

She gave me three keys, one for her own office (a vote of confidence, that!), one for Rudolf's, and one for the front door of the institute. I attached them to the ring with the key to Rudolf's apartment. "Now you have everything you need," she said.

But of course I had nothing. Absolutely nothing.

"May I take you out to dinner this evening?" I asked, a German once more. I would not have been surprised if she had blown me off with a burst of laughter.

She arranged to pick me up from the terrace at eight.

Chapter 5

IN HIS FINAL YEARS RUDOLF had been working like a madman (his word) on the novel that was to be his last. In a single great flash of brilliance, he meant to transform the genre itself and at the same time illuminate human nature in general through the singularity of his characters, after which double-lightning strike he would lapse quietly into his usual fog of despair. He had long been abnormally pessimistic about the future of our civilization and its culture, and since the more playful aspects of literature did not present enough of a challenge for him he felt that his final work must produce an ultimate salvation for humankind—something that was lacking in the intellectual output of the times. He spoke of fuel for the soul, inner self-illumination, using these pyromaniacal images to describe the explosion of literary fireworks that would be his last gift to the reading, thinking world.

But as he labored he saw no progress in his work, no development. "I am too old for ripening," went one of his illogical self-criticisms. Other writers are able to assess each new book in terms of their previous work, to see it as a building block in the edifice of their life's work—an edifice that will merely be completed by the last thing they write. Rudolf, who felt cheated of his youth, wanted his final work to be the entire castle; in other words, he wanted to pack everything into one great bundle. Since he refused to see his life in biographical terms, believing that such a formulaic conception of an individual's fate was either stupidity or naive delusion, he actually thought that he could do this, and that, moreover, this bundle would combust, in the temperate zone of our culture, like an incandescent meteorite. "Anyone who so much as touches my book must feel a continuous electrical current," he said once when he was on the verge of burning all his previous writings because he felt that they did not have enough "charge." In Rudolf's view, because we have been forced to give up the idea of immortality and no author could still be naive enough to believe that his works would outlive their legal copyright, this "thing"—the "bundle," the "prodigious glowing meteor"—would have to be assembled and detonated in a reasonably short time so that he could be around to enjoy the conflagration.

On the subject of contemporary literature he was excoriating, disparaging it as "middle-class prose." In particular, he detested the American novel, with its entangled family histories. An aunt sliding into insanity, a drunken father with a penchant for incest, a careworn housewife in love with the minister, a godforsaken landscape and some kids who just can't stand it: ordinary family chronicles, in other words, which to create one had only to observe and record the antics of one's neighbors—that was not what he understood by literature. The Origin and Propagation of Ill-Mannered Species was his Darwinian formulation for it. But even the more recent Italian and French authors were alien to him: rhetoricians who shamelessly appropriated Calvino's thinking, or sentimental windbags who adored the concept of the outsider, as if the outsider had not long since become passé. "Anyone who writes about outsiders these days is doomed to become one himself," he would say. "What irony, when what he really wants to be is a famous writer—an insider—nobly taking up the cudgels to defend the outsider. Have you ever known an outsider writer to challenge the establishment existentially in any way? No, he just gets more petit bourgeois, more ignorant, and more pathetic with every book, and that's the truth."

Of the German writers, there were a few that he liked, whom he corresponded with and invited to read at the institute, usually so that he could spend the afternoon with them beforehand. His introductory remarks at these readings were famous, because he praised the authors so ceremoniously, even reverently. He did go too far. "The distant embrace" was Elsa's comment, but to my mind that wasn't it. The praise was intentional—and he had invented for it an effusive language that did not exclude the melodramatic. Beyond that, he liked readings because they saved him the trouble of plowing through all those books on his own. Once the structure and meaning of a book became obvious to him—and that was often in the opening pages—he found it impossible to continue reading it, and would drop it somewhere and forget about it. But he was all ears when listening to the same book read by its author. Whenever I asked him what he was reading, he would reel off the titles of philosophical texts or volumes of theology, mostly research works I had never heard of. After the Internet became available, he ordered crates of books from all over the world, from rare-book dealers and small presses, with whom he maintained a regular electronic correspondence. It was astonishing, the things he knew. He kept in touch with every failed intellectual ever consigned to oblivion, and one might well wonder why, instead of writing sterile essays on communication, he did not write a history of intellectual rejects. A philosophical *salon des refusées:* everyone would have wanted to read a work on that subject, as written by Rudolf, the heresy specialist, whose own thinking could not be swayed by either persuasion or force. "That will all be part of my novel," he would say. That was now his answer to all questions. His gigantic work, his fiery meteor, would encompass all humanity's hidden, forgotten, discarded knowledge, which, he felt, remained in all of us, but which we no longer knew consciously because of the hegemony of representational reason, which he thought of as absolute unreason. "My *Faust,*" he would say on the telephone with a laugh, alluding to Valéry, whom he greatly admired. For, like Valéry, he was firmly convinced that all the problems that have been encountered in the course of the history of civilization, and been considered solved and put aside, must be reconsidered, for although out of sheer inertia we have ceased to think about them, they are critical to our survival. And, like Valéry, by his own reckoning he had filled hundreds of thick notebooks with his thoughts and ideas, which bit by bit he now wanted to feed into his novel. "Something like *The Man Without Qualities*?" I once asked him frivolously. Even then I suspected that he would never be able to finish this project. His answer was a snarl. All truly important works destroy their creators—that he was sure of. A few volumes, he said later, a few thousand pages—he was convinced that this really would be the world's last novel. He wanted to do away permanently with so-called imagination, which he blamed for the death of literature. Homer had no imagination, he used to say grandiosely, and even Dante's imagination had its limits, even if it did include heaven and hell. For him, imagination was a petit-bourgeois fad: since the death of metaphysics, everyone could claim some for himself. A writer praised for his imagination—he was a dead man for Rudolf. Politicians have to have imagination to package their lies, he would say, but for writers it is poison.

The title of the novel would be *The Testament.* I wasn't sure from what he told me whether it would be a novel in the old sense. The peculiar ideas Rudolf attached to this "monster," as he often called the work himself, pointed more in the direction of a large-scale, multipart essay. His aversion to fictional characters, from whom we are meant to learn whatever the author puts in their mouths, an aversion that had grown stronger in recent years, did not exactly lead one to expect a novel, however unconventional. Yet in the few, albeit lengthy, telephone conversations I had with him before his death he evinced a palpable loathing for all forms of avant-garde narrative, a growing fury at the destruction of the traditional narrative form, and since such a narrative must have characters, it was even harder to imagine that this novel would displace all previous ones. "Well, if you could imagine it," Rudolf then said matter-of-factly, "I wouldn't have to write it, would I?"

Sitting in Rudolf's office, I hardly knew where to begin my task, or how. Never was there an estate—literary or otherwise—with a more helpless, clueless executor. The high-ceilinged room, walled on all sides with bookshelves that extended even over the door, was reminiscent of a late-medieval *studiolo.* On the tiled floor, covered with frayed rugs, crates of more books had been deposited, some torn open, some sealed. The many tables ranged around the large desk served as repositories for piles of yet more books, and of folders bursting with newspaper clippings and manuscripts. A room filled with writing, a world perfect and complete and self-referential that absorbed and annihilated outside reality. And whatever space was not crammed with literature was occupied by a collection of objects that seemed to have been sitting there forever: glasses holding feathers and dried flowers; rocks; medicine bottles; a half-empty wine bottle in which a thick plug of mold had grown; countless photographs; toys (windup tin ducks made in China); keys to forgotten doors. A box of Magic Towels ("immersed in water briefly, it turns into a beautiful towel") imprinted with images of Mickey Mouse; next to that, a figurine of Hercules, missing its legs. How pale, uninteresting, and lifeless all this stuff becomes when the person who collected it is no longer around! These objects had been as precious to Rudolf as holy relics. Some of them I remembered from his novels: the old compasses, for instance, that one of his heroes demonstrates to a lover—the soul gone out of them now. There are writers who collect model trains or marbles; they invest these things with an exaggerated, mysterious importance, but the minute the author is dead his treasures end up in a junk shop, or coffined in a packing crate. When, decades later, grandchildren find this crate, they will puzzle over the relics their famous ancestor left behind: ivory cigarette-holders; old spectacles; ballpoint pens from Venice with tiny gondolas gliding sluggishly up and down inside them.

I picked up a small African wood carving of a naked man with an outsized head and two enormous Dumbo ears. It stood on top of a small projector displaying shots of Nice. Next was a Garamantian emerald, a chunk of stone from the Libyan desert. According to the display card, the "stone" was made of sand that melted when a comet, it is said, struck the desert north of Gilf Kebir, in Egypt, more than three million years ago. Tutankhamen had worn a scarab made of this material on his breast. I picked up the bright, translucent object in my hand and felt a frisson of heat run down my back. I remembered how oddly joyous Rudolf had been when he received this as a gift. For him, touching the piece was a sacred act, conquering time.

His desk was more or less in the same state as his study; it didn't look as if anyone had ever done any serious work at it. Only, in the one spot where he might have planted his elbows to prop up his tired head, the overflowing mountain of paper leveled out to a single thin sheet of cardboard, on which, carefully positioned, stood a packet of letter-size sheets of paper: a bit of order in the surrounding chaos.

I sat down and opened the packet. Its contents consisted of forty-two versions of one poem, which Rudolf had numbered in chronological order. All were handwritten in different colors of ink, in ballpoint pen, in pencil. In all of these media, Rudolf's affectedly ornate hand, in a sort of challenge to the graphology he had studied for years, retained a cool, calm look, as if certain that the object it was trying to catch would eventually end up in its net. It was an odd mixture of abrupt, jagged upstrokes and soft, looping downstrokes, as if he had practiced his penmanship in wet sand. The last, topmost version of the poem, signed and dated three days before Rudolf's death, was dedicated to me.

For M.

Tell the sparrow hawks
They must set the clock for me
At the hour of my death,
And the falcon, my friend,
Must shatter the dial
Before it is hit by lightning.
One statement lies hidden
In every friendship,
That is never spoken aloud,
Not once.
And so it was
Between us.

Grasping the paper with clammy fingers, I felt an overpowering, withering sadness creep over me. My neck stiffened, my breathing became shallow: sadness like an illness that had been lying in wait for me. The few words that Rudolf kept rearranging in the last months of his life were his real final work, his testament, written for me. And why for me? We had only spoken on the phone of late, and even then he had been ill-tempered and unwilling to answer my questions. Instead, each of these attempts at communication—all of them initiated by me—had evolved into a long monologue in which Rudolf tried to justify his life and his writing. Finally, he would interrupt himself. "It can't turn out well if we focus on ourselves too intensively," he would say. "A man revealed is a lost man. Let us have him keep his dimness, his darkness, his imperfections, and not destroy him through literature."

I had made the calls, I had been the one who wanted to talk. It was due to me that our connection did not break off like so many of his other friendships. I'd always thought that perhaps inside this big, bristly-haired man hid a shy, awkward child, as he had been when I first met him in Berlin.

I had just finished my printing apprenticeship and was looking for a job. Meanwhile, since I couldn't afford to stay in the apartment on my own, I also had to find a roommate. Back then I was unable to deal with the world on my own. I had decided that the revolution everyone talked of was stupid and dishonest, though a belief in it would have neatly freed me from my youthful self-recriminations. The world took no notice of me, but I didn't want to just stand there on the sidelines, watching it, so I decided to find a companion.

My advertisement was answered by a literature student, who called on the phone and told me—in a horrendous Swabian dialect, stringing words out one by one, with long pauses—that he was writing a dissertation on Kafka's diaries for Professor Emrich at the Free University of Berlin. In the evenings when I got home from my various part-time jobs, he would read to me from it while I made us something to eat. *Schriftsteller reden Gestank:* "Writers' talk stinks." That's one aperçu of Kafka's I will never forget.

Rudolf himself never cooked. He wasn't even willing or able to do the paltry errands required to assemble our spartan meals. I had to lug everything, including the water and the wine, up the five flights by myself. It was almost unbearable, the way he played the role of the serious man making himself ready for an important life. While I washed the dishes, he remained seated at the kitchen table, smoking and reading aloud, totally self-absorbed, heaving an occasional sigh, as if Kafka's own spirit had entered into him. This revolutionary pessimist was always behind with the rent, too, even though he had received a generous fellowship from the university. When I reproached him for it, a roguish smile would cross his usually masklike face, dismissive of rich Philistines whose only thoughts were of money. Once a month he invited his friends to our place, always at a time when he could count on my being flush enough to pay for the food. On those occasions he was a perfect host, concerned with the well-being of his friends, to whom he sang my praises as a delightful landlord and a wonderful cook. It also fell to me to run out and get more wine from the local bar, so that nothing need interrupt Rudolf's endless talk about the cataclysmic changes that must revolutionize the study of German literature. Actually, I was happy to escape on an errand: these polemical discussions gave me the creeps. When Rudolf digressed to hold forth about a materialistic interpretation of Goethe's poetry, a chill would run down my spine. In company, the subtle, sensitive Kafka reader metamorphosed into a dogmatic blowhard who enjoyed forcing everyone to listen to his enigmatic pronouncements. This was hardly the open, unforced thinking he was urging me to adopt.

Among Rudolf's worthy audience were some of the many female fellow students who were smitten with him, and one of these guests, who occupied our kitchen as if it were a seminar room, would frequently spend the night. When I got up the next morning on these occasions, the exhausted philosopher would still be asleep, while Eva, Christa, or Dagmar would be back in the kitchen, her elbows on the table and her head in her hands, waiting for me to serve the coffee. His admirers were just as incapable as he was of doing anything except their studies. Eva, in particular, who was the only child of wealthy parents and expected a big inheritance, was grateful for my attentiveness, which relieved her of the need to wait upon herself. When Rudolf left the city after completing his dissertation, she continued her visits, sitting at the kitchen table with her notes for a paper on Veronese before her, until in the evening I saw to it that she did not faint from hunger. After I left Berlin myself, to seek my misfortune in London, her parents (Papa was a big shot at Siemens, Mama a management consultant) took over the lease on my apartment, so that their daughter would not be subjected to the distractions of moving. Eva is now a professor of art history at Braunschweig, settled into a humdrum marriage; she spends her summer vacations at her *finca* on Ibiza, preparing for the rigors of a new semester. And she, after first calling me, would occasionally call Rudolf in Italy; he, in Turin, would immediately call me, up in arms about being bothered by the thoroughly uninspired Eva. I have no idea what happened to Christa and Dagmar.

The last woman to join our helpless kitchen crew had been Elsa, the daughter of a man from Lecce in Apulia, one of our original foreign guest workers, who had been decorated for his pioneering role by the German president. His first job had been at the Opel factory in Rüsselsheim; he had subsequently opened a pizzeria in the provincial town of Salzgitter that eventually became a chain, with franchises throughout the Harz Mountain area. He died in circumstances that were officially unresolved, but in fact everyone knew that he had been killed by the Mafia for refusing to pay protection money. Elsa's mother had died of grief soon after. The pizza chain was sold, and the money fell into the laps of the two daughters: one invested in a gourmet food shop in Munich; the other, Elsa, invested in a professor on the make—Rudolf—who used the money to buy the heaps of first editions that now surrounded me. Did she have any idea then what she had gotten herself involved in?

Rudolf never had much to say about Elsa. She exists, he sometimes said. And when she answered the phone, which was seldom enough, you didn't get much more than that out of her. She had written two widely translated studies about a Spanish heretical sect that had earned her a teaching position at the university, but in the last years, after Rudolf began raking in money from his novels, you didn't hear much about her. Probably her major activity had been cleaning up the terrace.

The Testament: So was that it? A stack of paper with forty-two drafts of a little poem? I felt as if I were bolted to that chair where Rudolf had sat for more than twenty years—a creaky old thing that lurched every which way when I moved, balking at being of any further support to anyone. It now dawned on me that it wasn't Elsa or his book or his students that Rudolf had abandoned but me. I was the one who had been left behind—at least, that was how I chose to interpret the sadness I felt. He had bid farewell to everyone else over the course of his life, step by step, tentatively yet clearly feeling his way, pulling back inch by inch until he reached that last wall, and then vanishing irrevocably. There was something spooky about the way he had isolated himself. He had done it patiently, decorously, moving in an enclosed space from which he never found his way out. The more monstrous this creation became, the surer Rudolf must have been that he would never master it. Elsa had known how close he was to the edge, ready to jump at any time; his students had grown accustomed to his never being available. But he had ditched *me* with a suddenness that even he must have deplored; otherwise he would not have sat at that poem for weeks on end, like the Polish writer,

Jan Potocki, who kept on polishing an iron ball until it finally fit into the barrel of his gun, which he then used to shoot himself. Rudolf had quite clearly postponed his death until he was happy with the poem: he had written it and fiddled with it and improved it, all with death in mind. Why hadn't he written another forty drafts, four hundred, four thousand, and given me some time?

The anger that was now beginning to take over my grief was interrupted by a clanking noise. It was eight o'clock, so that had to be Marta at the door. But before I could rise from the treacherous chair, leaving grief and anger behind, I heard steps in the corridor, and I was still zigzagging around the stacks of books when I caught a whiff of cigarette smoke and turned around to find her already standing in the room. Like an animal, I thought, that knows every hiding place in the apartment, can disappear at the first sign of danger, and reappears as soon as there's something it can grab and run off with. She must have lit her cigarette in her office, even though this was strictly forbidden, for the trip upstairs. She looked for an ashtray, and, not finding one, dropped the butt into a test tube—there were a couple on the desk, set in a wooden rack. She held her thumb over the opening until the glass took on a milky color and the butt went out. Then she put the tube back in its place. Her cavalier self-assurance in that place left me speechless. Nor was she surprised at *my* surprise. To cap her little performance—did she expect me to applaud?—she sat down in Rudolf's chair, where I had just been sitting, and asked me if I had any questions.

I was still somewhat disoriented, I told her. Without any clear idea of this extensive apartment's layout, I had had to feel my way around in the dark, dodging the intimidating furniture that had been gathered within this dungeon. After much groping I had finally happened on the kitchen, beyond which lay Rudolf's study. Each room I opened along the way had greeted me with a musty smell, a dull, stale odor that was more intense in Rudolf's lair, for one thing because the room had no windows, and for another because the books in it had been shedding dust for ages. Strange that Rudolf, who in his later years had liked nothing better than to talk about long walks that others had taken, by using old maps had painstakingly figured out the hiking paths that Pavese, to escape his own suffocating melancholia, had followed through the hills around Turin. Strange, I thought, that Rudolf, a late-blooming naturalist, Rudolf, of all people, had immured himself and all his knowledge inside that cave, even though the apartment had plenty of bright, light-filled rooms. Perhaps he had needed its absolute silence. In the end, he used to say, the only second in the day that counts is the one in which you hear nothing, not the grinding of the great cosmic noise or the little deadly noises, but nothing, and this moment is the payback for all your suffering—he could, and did, say such things, as if trying to prepare himself for that one second of silence.

After finding the light switch, I had at first remained standing in the doorway, since I was not sure whether I should just blithely walk into Rudolf's sanctuary without an invitation from Rudolf himself, but then, after getting a little more used to the oppressive odor, I had started moving along the bookshelves, in the general direction of the desk, though any moment I expected to be stopped by a human voice, and continually started at the creaking sound of the heavy wooden floorboards underfoot. Taking short steps, on tiptoe, so as not to disturb the order of this little cell, I had finally made it to the desk, an explorer coming to an oasis after a long trek in an unpopulated wilderness. Thank goodness for the chair, which I knew more or less personally, since Rudolf had discovered and acquired it in my presence, in a secondhand shop in Rome. I had eased myself carefully into it and remained sitting there until Marta's arrival.

Now Marta volunteered to be our Ariadne, as she put it, for a short tour of the labyrinth. Going through the doorway, she brushed up against me slightly. I was wondering whether this brief but perceptible contact was intentional when I heard her voice from rather farther away. "Here we have Elsa's office," she said, tapping on a closed door. "This is the dining room, almost never used, since Rudolf preferred to eat in the kitchen; over there was his bedroom, and here the little parlor, the guest room, Elsa's bedroom, a bigger parlor, the laundry room." Finally, we found ourselves at the iron gate that led to the terrace, where she stopped. Marta had the annoying habit of turning on every light switch we came to, and immediately turning it off again, so that I seemed to be viewing the apartment under strobe lights, and by the time we returned to the kitchen I had forgotten which room was where. Her "tour" had been designed to keep me in total confusion. She was starting to get my goat: loud, self-confident, she had taken control without the slightest hesitation, not only of the institute but of its late director's private residence as well. Watching her operate, you would never have suspected that just hours ago, at the cemetery, she had bidden Rudolf farewell.

"You'll be sleeping in Rudolf's bed, by the way," she said, as she showed me the way back to his room. Casually, over her shoulder, she added, "I have spread out all his papers in the guest room, so you can work in peace." She had not wanted, she explained, to spread them out on Rudolf's bed; it would have been rather inhuman, because that was where, at the end, he had most liked to work himself, she assured me. It had been quite an effort for her to move them all. Sometimes it had taken her an eternity to find on that bed some official papers or other that he was supposed to have looked at, and all the while he had sat there, unperturbed, scribbling away on his wooden writing plank.

"I was the only person he ever allowed into his bedroom," she said in conclusion. "He banished everyone else."

I suddenly remembered a trip to Tunis that I had made with Rudolf and Elsa in the late seventies, to escape the Christmas holidays. We had barely landed, after a horrible flight, when we were informed that violent demonstrations were in progress, because of the rising cost of bread, and we were whisked off to a hotel, which we were not allowed to leave. This was no beachfront property; it was right in the middle of the city, and had no air-conditioning and no restaurant. We were forced to share our room with an American couple, both geologists with a considerable amount of equipment, which took up the greater part of the room's limited space. Rudolf was more than usually forthcoming on first meeting them, but his tentative amicability turned to hostility when the question arose of who would sleep in the bed and who would sleep on mattresses on the floor. A compromise, arrived at after a lengthy and somewhat unpleasant discussion in which reflections on all of the involuntary cellmates' physical attributes played a decisive role, provided that on the first night Rudolf and the female geologist would share the double bed, which was worn out in every sense, while Elsa and the male geologist would each put down a mattress on the side, and I would get the space at the foot. The next day we would switch. Meanwhile, shots and shouting could be heard from the street; police sirens howled all night. Calm was restored after three days, and we immediately flew back home, while the Americans took off for the south. Later, Rudolf worked this episode into his second novel: the erotic embellishments that his readers found so amusing were totally invented. Since I hadn't slept a wink all three nights (partly out of fear, partly because Rudolf snored dreadfully), I knew for a fact that there had been no intimacies. There had been no switching, either. For the entire three days, Rudolf had lain in his original share of that bed and worked, and on the first evening he more or less had the whole of it under occupation. But when after dinner—which had to be sent for—he deposited his dishes on the American woman's side, things got violent. Their faces distorted with rage, the two geologists heaved Rudolf's dishes, notebooks, and writing implements back onto his half of the bed and proceeded to fill in the gap between the twin mattresses with their long, narrow instrument cases, a frontier that Rudolf respected.

Thinking about it now made me laugh out loud. Marta, always one step ahead, looked back at me quizzically and said, "Believe it or not, I really was the only one allowed to enter his bedroom."

Chapter 6

WE DINED AT A LITTLE TRATTORIA near the institute. Marta had suggested sending out for Chinese, but I wanted to get out of that building at all costs. I don't think I could have swallowed a mouthful inside it, especially after our trip to the terrace. Seeing poor old Caesar, now almost bald, half blind, and so severely arthritic that he could move only with great effort, had been too much. While the birds shrieked and chattered around us, he had come crawling up, tail feebly wagging, as if he remembered me, but the instant my hand touched his scabrous, hairless skin he had collapsed into a miserable heap.

"Watch out, he stinks like hell," said Marta matter-of-factly as always—(or did she just pretend to be?) and left me with the wretched, gasping dog, while she brought food and fresh water to the other animals, some of them visible, others only audible. I could hear her tending to them on the other side of the dense wall of plants, but could offer her no help, because Caesar had rolled onto my feet with the full weight of his grief. Was I sorry for him?

It is so easy to lavish sympathy on animals, since we don't really understand them. But either he really had recognized me or he thought I was Rudolf—which was fine with me and, for a minute, made me happy. He furrowed his warty brow and looked toward me mutely with his filmy, mustard-colored eyes, a dying king. I couldn't speak to him—I had no words fit to console him. Instead, the chatty plants did the talking. Every gust of wind coaxed a whisper from the broad palm fronds, and from the reeds, which had grown particularly well on the terrace, given its ingenious irrigation system. A strange paradise Rudolf had devised and then abandoned.

"Poor beasts," I heard Marta mutter. "Left here all alone by your famous German author! From here on, things will improve, just be patient." A strange woman, Marta. She made me feel that I hadn't understood a thing about this great tragedy. And what good were my literary executive privileges if I never got to the core of real-life drama?

Just as I was wondering what she meant by "improve," worrying about what would really happen to these animals, she came up behind me and tapped me on the shoulder. In her off-the-cuff manner, she ordered me to leave the terrace with her; the animals, too, needed some peace.

Hadn't Elsa taken care of the terrace? I asked, as we stood, ducking slightly, in the heavy iron gateway that separated Rudolf's strange Eden from the civilized corruptions of the rest of the building.

Ah, Elsa . . . Given the situation, Marta didn't want to say any more on the subject.

At the trattoria I ate and drank more than usual, both because I was hungry and because I could hardly get a word in edgewise. Every one of my brief questions elicited a long-winded, self-important torrent of words, and whenever I asked for the slightest elucidation of anything Marta said I got an answer that was twice as long and even harder to understand. I was being initiated into the secrets of Turin—with a vengeance.

I had worked my way through almost everything on the menu and nearly finished a second bottle of wine, and still there was no sign that our one-sided conversation might be ending anytime soon. Yet I found myself absorbing every nasty anecdote, every shameless rumor, with an eagerness that disturbed me. Sometimes I had the impression I had never met the Rudolf that Marta was talking about, but then glimpsed his tortured face peeping out from behind her stage curtain of words, his gestures mutely signaling me not to believe everything that was being said about him.

The main question, of course, was whether and how much I could trust Marta. If I took at face value everything she was telling me, with her air of utter frankness and emotional unrestraint, in a voice that must have been audible in every corner of the crowded restaurant, I would have to believe that Rudolf had long since given up on his novel. To be sure, Marta said, he had continued to work on the project, producing mountains of notes that she would collect several times a day from every room he worked in, but especially from his bedroom and his bed in the morning; still, it had long since been clear to her, and of course to him, that this enormous pile of index cards would never, ever, become a coherent book. On the other hand (and here, as she so often did, she slipped in one of her unpleasant and inappropriate expressions), you knew him well enough to know that, unlike many of his colleagues, especially the German ones, he simply would never have published the book as an interesting collection of notes and passed it off as the invention of a new genre. He knew that he was writing for the trash can.

I left this pronouncement unanswered, as I had the others of its kind, and took a big gulp of Piedmont wine, so that she wouldn't read my lack of reaction as a protest. Not only had she just informed me that her German was not as good as my Italian, but also I knew that this particular school of German authors, which Rudolf had loved and which she claimed to despise, had never been translated into Italian. She was talking, in her overbearing way, of matters she didn't and couldn't know anything about. In truth, she was clearly even less solid than I had at first assumed, and in all innocence I started wondering how Rudolf, who was usually bored stiff by common literary chatter, could have put up with her wholesale nonsense. As she talked on, there was a hint of challenge in her eyes, yet it was continually being displaced by some great unhappiness. What could it be? I felt sorry for her, to my annoyance. Was Marta just aggrandizing herself at Rudolf's expense, or did she mean to give me, his executor, a clear signal about how I should read and evaluate the pile of manuscripts that awaited me? Had Rudolf ever once hinted that he could no longer handle this material, or had he ever said, even jestingly, that he would have to invent a new genre if he was to be able to publish his "monster," since even in its unfinished state it was "interesting" enough to shock and awe the public? *Interesting, more or less interesting, interesting in parts, but a failure as a whole . . .* this was how he had described books that held no interest for him whatsoever. *Interesting* meant *horrible, torturous, boring;* if a writer decided to be interesting, Rudolf said, he was lost to literature. Art must dispense with everything that is interesting, he maintained, must strive for no "effect" not inherent in the words themselves. Were Beckett's novels *interesting*? Was Ad Reinhardt, one of his favorite painters, *interesting*? Artistes manqués, who themselves have nothing to offer, naturally seek out the company of *interesting* people. Writers who meet publicly with politicians and then write about it wish to make themselves *interesting.* "Has René Char ever said anything on the problem of abortion," he once asked me laughingly, during one of our telephone calls. "Did Günter Eich meddle in Adenauer's tax legislation? No, he simply moved to Austria to escape taxes!"

Whenever anyone in Germany asked Rudolf to raise his voice for or against someone or something, he always called me up for advice, even though it was 90 percent certain from the outset that he would refuse to participate in almost any form of solidarity. "Why doesn't anybody ever demonstrate *for* something?" he would snarl at me, the mere conveyor of the request. I often caught myself thinking that as his deputy I should write something for him, so that by proxy, at least, he could play a role in certain political events.

His political abstinence in later years stood in sharp contrast to his behavior in his ultra-Marxist youth. Despite his close collaboration with Professor Emrich, Rudolf had been the fair-haired boy of the left-wing Germanists at the Free University—an intimidating group of bookish zealots who, against their own inbred convictions, advocated nutty ideas that later no one was allowed to remind them of. Such things were no longer talked about. Politics was the turf of idiots now. But still, it became known through the usual leaks that large sums of money, resulting from well-placed sales of the movie rights to his books, had flowed to certain political organizations, although since more often than not I had been the messenger of these secret transactions, I had sworn—and kept—an oath never to breathe a word of this to anyone. Rudolf would do practically anything to avoid giving the impression that he wanted to be *interesting*.

Marta, on the other hand, did want to make herself *interesting* and knew how to do it. Since Elsa was now totally "off line," as Marta put it (Elsa had long since written off Rudolf's book, and apparently done all she could to keep Rudolf from working on it), under the circumstance that is, of her being "off line" (Marta must have wished to emphasize the banality of the description by repeating it), she, Marta, was the only person with whom Rudolf had discussed the project—except for me, of course. Clearly Rudolf must have exchanged a word or two on the subject with me now and then, at least on the phone. What Marta was really saying was that in this respect she and I were both co-authors of the *Testament*, Rudolf's *Testament*, and since she assumed that I understood my own role she wanted me to see hers in the proper light as well. She wanted to have a contract with me.

I was speechless. I nodded mechanically, I smoked my cigarette and drank my wine in silence. Despite my lavish dinner, I felt empty, nothing inside me but a freezing void. Marta's last words fell into this void with a thud, like a load of coal in a dark cellar. Before she could hijack any more of the evening, I made a last effort to interrupt her monologue and succeeded, paid the check, got up, tired and swaying like a drunkard, and walked out of the restaurant with her.

Chapter 7

I DIDN'T WANT TO WAKE UP. Not quite knowing where I was or under what circumstances I had fallen asleep, I buried my aching skull in the hollow of the threadbare pillow, then rolled over onto my stomach, enfolding the pillow in my arms. All the while I kept my eyes shut, even though every sound and smell all but commanded that I stop pretending I was somewhere else. I was lying in Rudolf's bed, there was no denying it any longer. Sleep! I had to have a little more sleep. But how much more? Just one more minute! The scraps of dreams floating in my head were so much more peaceful and comforting than reality, whose shock troops had marched implacably to the margins of my consciousness and were now poised to invade its center, that I was determined to summon up all my willpower to hold the enemy off. Instead, of course, I ended by opening my eyes in surrender. The muscle that moves the eyelid works harder than any other muscle of the body, relative to its size; even in marathon runners. Comforting myself with this useless bit of information, I decided to look my misfortune in the face.

Marta was busy pulling up blinds and opening windows. She had left a tray with a pot of coffee and croissants on the night table. Two croissants and two cups, no saucers; a few stray cubes of sugar. Would she put the sugar in the cups, as I always did, before she poured the coffee? For obvious reasons I could not suggest this: modesty, with its thousand shackles, held me back.

"You sleep even more soundly than your friend Rudolfo," she said, after I had finally hunched myself up to a sitting position, covering myself to the neck with the bedsheet that served as a spread. Whatever she said, her voice retained that peculiar mixture of objective intonation and imperative urgency that had annoyed me throughout the previous evening. It was there even in what she didn't say. "It's time you got up": she didn't put this into words, but she looked as if she were thinking it.

The mention of Rudolf's name had jolted me wide awake. Hadn't Rudolf continually complained of his insomnia, which he nonetheless praised for allowing him, in spite of the demands of his allegedly time-consuming and demeaning university tasks, to continue with his literary work? "You have to train yourself to do without sleep," he had advised me on more than one occasion, when I complained about not being able to get any work done outside my job. "Too much sleep is unhealthy and anticapitalist—three hours ought to be enough." For I, too, had tried my hand at literary work, writing a few essays that had gained me some notice among my colleagues, but all my attempts at writing fiction had never produced much beyond a compromise novella or a fragment of a full-length novel, never more than fifty pages. My books were doomed by my weariness and my constant sense of shame—a lifelong deep shame at saying anything at all, at making anything public. I have never even understood why I should tell God anything, since, presumably, he already knew it. Better not to speak, or to speak only to oneself, in secret. Better to think in silence. But it was being tired that ultimately made me lose interest in my characters, who after twenty pages would begin acting neglected, feeling abandoned, and eventually just fade away. Evaporate. They would move to the country, pursue their career of being failures, and never return. Their unhappiness bothered me, and I was pleased when they didn't stick around. As a result, they always ended by withdrawing their trust in me. In the evenings I was too drained to recall them to action, and just let them go AWOL. Rudolf, on the other hand, claimed that he started writing after midnight, up there on the terrace with the animals, and only called it quits after sunrise. "You have got to keep your eye on your characters for seven or eight hours at a stretch, otherwise they will get up to no good and dump you," he said. Yet he always spoke with respect of the short sessions Thomas Mann (whom he otherwise had not thought much of) devoted daily to his writing. Now here was Marta telling me that "Rudolfo," like me, had been a heavy sleeper. Suddenly one of my stories popped into my mind, another that I hadn't been able to finish because the hero, if I can call him that, never found his way home again. This was the true story of an uncle of mine who had taken up marathon running to cure his insomnia and who had never come back from a run he started in Egypt around the Pyramids. I have photos that show him as part of the crowd, but sometime after that he'd vanished. Since he had lived by himself, my family had to mourn him alone.

Marta sat on the edge of the bed, put a lump of sugar ("Like last night? Rudolfo always took two in the morning!") into one of the small brown espresso cups, and poured coffee over it. Since I made no move to reach for a croissant, she took one and tore it into little sections and handed them to me, forced them on me, practically, so that I had no choice but to bite into the fragile pastry—I normally like the unfilled type, but not in bed—with the predictable result that there was soon a wreath of crumbs on the sheet, which in turn gave Marta a chance to clean up the mess, which she did with quick, sweeping strokes of the hand. She had probably practiced this courtesy with Rudolf often.

"I've set you up with three desks. This one here"—she pointed to a narrow, dark, stained one by the window—"the desk in the guest room, and the desk in his office downstairs, at the institute. And of course you can use the one on the terrace, after ten, at least, when the girls are through feeding the animals. One of the girls stays until two and takes care of the plants, but that shouldn't disturb you. I have to ask you not to use Elsa's room for your work. Above all, we have to avoid mixing their papers up. Here"—she pointed again, this time at a carefully stacked mountain of gray cardboard cartons—"I have compiled that portion of the literary estate that Rudolf himself had begun to organize; you can start with that. I will show you everything else later."

She was in a hurry, she said, because she had to take care of Rudolf's students, who by now were downstairs "probably breaking the door down."

I remained in Rudolf's bed until she left, huddled up, waiting for the sound of the apartment door. As soon as I heard the muffled thud, I jumped out of bed, totally naked, as I now realized to my horror, and raced to the bedroom door to lock it from the inside. Since I first opened my eyes, I had needed to pee, thanks no doubt to those two bottles of inferior wine, and so I hurried through the dark, quiet apartment searching for a bathroom, passing shadowy mirrors weakly reflecting my pale green features, until, having opened and closed half a dozen doors, I finally found what I was looking for.

I could not enjoy the cool quiet of the dark-blue-tiled bathroom for long, however, for now an explosive crashing sound could be heard, followed by loud, chirping voices. These came, it soon developed, from two Thai housemaids, who had unlocked the bathroom door but had been prevented from entering by the safety chain. They walked past me toward the kitchen, murmuring *"Buon giorno"* while I stood there speechless, wrapped in a hastily grabbed hand towel. As I watched their retreat from behind, my hand still on the doorknob, the telephone on the desk just outside the bathroom started ringing. Marta. Had I let the girls in? Yes. Was I at work yet? No. Could she give me a hand? No. OK, talk to you later.

I groped my way back to Rudolf's bedroom and lay down again. I needed to recover from the breathlessness of the past twenty-four hours, the unaccustomed rapid pace of events, Marta's unstoppable logorrhea, the mysterious circumstances that had brought me to this bed in the first place, the significance of the assignment awaiting me—Elsa's request that I look through and evaluate Rudolf's literary estate, a request conveyed over the phone but by no means fixed in writing. And then the short notice on which I had started my journey and the urgency attending my arrival, when Elsa, two days after Rudolf's death and three days before his burial, had suffered some kind of stroke, the severity of which was at first unclear but had since been recognized as critical. Thoughts of these events and the problems they posed had set off a violent commotion in my skull, already devastated by that sulfite-soaked wine. All things considered, I was certain that I could make sense of the situation only in repose.

Impossible. Now that I was awake, I found, I just couldn't stay lying in bed. So I shuffled back to the bathroom to brush my teeth with Rudolf's (or Elsa's) toothbrush. I had not yet had a chance to pick up my luggage from the railway checkroom where I had left it. My dead friend's toothbrush. A red, ragged, travel-maimed thing, a Dr. Best model with squashed bristles that pierced my gums unpleasantly. I remembered how much it had annoyed me in the old days when my brilliant roommate blithely used my toothbrush, whenever his own got too worn, even for him, and how despite my protests it took him days to get a new one. He had one particularly revolting habit: using my toothbrush not just to brush his teeth but also to clean off his tongue, which was coated every morning with a thick layer of slime, the result of his poor diet and excessive smoking. This slime could be removed from the bristles only by a special procedure, which Rudolf in his haste was happy to leave to me. The sadistic streak he doubtless indulged was further encouraged by the disgust it caused me, and the more openly I showed my revulsion the worse his insults became. The exalted manner in which he would dissect my bourgeois squeamishness, the obnoxious, supercilious way that he would later hand me a new toothbrush, so I would never have to put the old one he had polluted back into my mouth, this kind of nastiness had abated in recent years but never completely disappeared. He would torment me during our telephone calls with every trick in the book; for instance, he would accuse me of loving life too much, of wanting to create order while he was dangling over the abyss, and would ridicule all notions that order was even possible as a theater of illusion. Toward the end, he accused me of using the telephone to spy on him. "You want to know what I think," he shouted into the receiver, "in order to control me, but I think nothing!"

Now, having outlived him, I had his toothbrush bristles in my teeth once more and listened, foaming at the mouth, to his commentary: "Fine, you're in great shape, no big deal for you to get up in the morning, see yourself in the mirror, stick my toothbrush in your mouth and have a great day, while the worms are gnawing the flesh from my bones."

As so often happens when you are in a strange house, everything I did took longer, much longer than usual. I walked around the house aimlessly, heard strange noises, looked out the window, watched the pigeons do nothing, and forgot about the coffee, so that the tiny coffeemaker nearly exploded and I had to cool the thing off under cold water and fill it back up again. Where were the cups, where did he keep the sugar, why aren't there any teaspoons? The tyranny of daily life comes into its own in strange households. Finally, when all my frittering and fiddling was done, after I had returned to Rudolf's bedroom, made the bed, and dressed myself in yesterday's clothes, which reeked of Marta's cigarettes, and calmed down, I was ready to give my attention to the mountains of cartons, scribbled all over with Rudolf's familiar handwriting, that took up most of the right-hand side of the room. Sixty-four cartons, carefully stacked, the edges of the ones on the bottom a bit squashed by the weight of the ones on top. Arranged as Projects, Letters, Works Completed, Works Not Completed, Documents. The thought of having to look through this mass of paper made me anything but happy. Can what is real be contained in documents, found in bygone writings? The innocence of the novice, the tentative progress, the sure sensibilities of the mature writer, the crises and long dry periods—all of that was stacked up in front of me. A writer's life. Where should I begin?

I was just about to remove the first carton from the top row when I heard the tripping step of one of the Thai girls, who in her birdlike voice chirped something like "Have a nice day" at me and disappeared without another sound. And I had not quite lifted the papers out of their box when the door opened again, this time to reveal Marta, who had come to check on my progress.

"You won't find much in that box," she said, after taking a quick peek over my shoulder.

I couldn't stand her being so close to me. Would she always be listening, from now on, whenever I communed with my dead friend? Rudolf had been exaggeratedly distant and discreet in his dealings with others: how had he endured this drill sergeant of a woman? I was reminded of the fate of poor Peter Kien, the hero of Canetti's *Auto da Fé,* who, to buy himself a kind of distance through a deliberate closeness, had married his dictatorial, hateful housekeeper, and naturally come to a dreadful end. Rudolf loved that novel; he talked about Peter Kien as one talks about a close friend. The longer I stood there, gawking at the carton, with Marta at my back, the more urgently I wished to flee to Germany with all these boxes and bring Rudolf back to his home country. I had to extricate these gray cartons, his life's work, from this woman's hands, wrest them from her influence, keep them from her sight.

As if Marta had sensed that I was about to jam the cover back onto these documents that had just seen the light of day, she grabbed the carton from the side and simply turned it upside down, spreading its entire contents before me in one fell swoop.

"So you see, nothing special," she said. "Nothing that would be of interest to posterity."

As fast as I could I pressed both hands down on the small stack of paper, to keep her from clawing it apart, and pleaded with her to let me get to work.

"If you keep up this pace you might as well add on your own literary estate," she said, and laughed in my face. "Rudolfo often said it was your indecisiveness that kept you from getting down to writing. But in one hour you have to give the university president your first report, and if by then you've only got through Rudolf's old travel documents he will start to doubt your competence."

Competence, how I hated that word. But I had in fact agreed to give the president a report on Rudolf's literary leavings, because the university and the city of Turin had both declared their willingness to house the papers in a special archive that would be set up exclusively for Rudolf's life and work. Elsa had therefore suggested that I, as one of the people most familiar with his writing, be his literary executor, and my findings would determine whether the estate should remain in Turin or be taken to Germany, where, at the time of Rudolf's death, both the state archive at Marbach and the mayor of his hometown had signaled their readiness to accept it. In all likelihood, neither Marbach nor the hometown had any idea of the size of this legacy, for we were not talking about the twenty or thirty boxes of manuscripts, letters, notebooks, and documents that generally comprise the residue of an author's life. Rudolf's manic compulsion to write, combined with the excerpts he made from other works, had formed a corpus of paper that would probably fill several rooms, and, of course, his library also belonged with his work. If the library were to be separated from the work, then all his papers might as well be destroyed, since without his books they made no sense. For instance, besides his voluminous scripts on "Pascal's Pathology," there were shelves devoted solely to his own collected notes on Resentment, Greed, and Shame; he wanted to write extensive monographs on these phenomena, which he found more meaningful than terms like Society and Economy. The marked-up photocopies, dictated passages, and handwritten notes were stored along with more than a hundred books on each of these topics. Here was material for an extensive, multivolume complete edition, taking shape before my eyes as a published work, and furnished with a detailed afterword by me.

The university administrators, in their interview with Elsa the day after Rudolf's death, had pointed out that the papers in both the university office and the institute's offices, subject to court examination, were the property of the Italian state, a point that Elsa, in her confused and depressed condition, had not disputed. Since I knew nothing of Italian administrative law and had no intention of involving myself in these complicated matters, I had suggested to Elsa that she keep both offices locked for the time being. On the one hand, I argued, she should be happy that there was such strong public interest in Rudolf's literary testament—which on the Italian side, at least, surprised me, since Rudolf had never had anything good to say about the university administration—but on the other hand we had to do everything we possibly could to prevent those papers from his office having nothing to do with university matters from falling into the wrong hands. In this curious struggle for the literary legacy of this newly departed man, absolutely nothing could be done without Elsa's permission, but what would happen if, for reasons I dared not think about, Elsa were to be permanently bedridden—aside from any other eventualities? While Marta stood there, I silently and solemnly swore to myself that, whatever happened, my talk with the president would be just between him and me, and that I would insist on being allowed to pursue my work without supervision. All keys handed over, no more breakfasts in bed, total solitude.

"Should I make you some coffee?" asked Marta, who apparently had earned a diploma in face and mind reading. "Do you want to meet with the president down in my office or up here?"

"Here," I said, with a promptness that seemed weird even to me, and tapped on the documents in front of me like a regular literary executor. "Here, and nowhere else, if you don't mind."

"*Bene*" was her two-syllable answer. And before going into the kitchen to make me another coffee she remade the bed, muttering audibly to herself that the president didn't really have to know who had spent the night in it.

I acted as if I hadn't heard, although inside I was so wound up that I was ready to explode, and the minute Marta left I jumped up from my chair and ran through the darkening apartment, yelling, cursing. This know-it-all arrogant woman, who steered me and our conversation as she chose—her condescending manner and obnoxious allusions were bringing me to the boiling point. I am too meek to deal with these supercool professional bureaucrats, too trusting, too naive—in short, nowhere near ballsy enough.

On the other hand, of course, she was right. For if I let things go on as they were, let her lead me around like a fool, in the few days I had I would barely be able even to look through all the material properly, let alone come to a decision about it.

I had to find some quiet, stay calm, and get to work.

Chapter 8

I COULDN'T SIT DOWN. It was simply out of the question for me to settle myself in the chair in which Rudolf had sat himself to death. His calamity, his will to unhappiness, had somehow become part of this chair; it was still warm with unhappiness. Sitting here, leafing nervously through his papers, trying to uncover a reason for it all, would feel like inadmissible meddling, even desecration, since I knew only a laughably tiny segment of Rudolf's life, so every piece of paper would have to contain a revelation. What had he eaten, where had he stayed, had he traveled first-class? Whom had he met, what had he noticed? Exactly when had he begun his journey into loneliness, when had he formed an alliance with Pascal against his friends? Would I find a confession? A beggar whom Rudolf had admired once said that confessions are clearest when they are recanted. And what would Rudolf have done if someone had told him that he had just ten days to get his literary estate in order? A few years back, I might have answered that Rudolf would have destroyed all of it, trashed it, burned it. Yes, burned it. Then we could have placed beside the urn containing his own ashes one filled with the ashes of his written remains, and between them a stack of his published works. As for his library, he would have turned it over to an antiquarian book dealer he knew, to be dispersed among books that others had left behind, to become absorbed and therefore invisible.

What dreadful responsibility had I been delegated? Weren't there experts around, executors with a more practiced eye who could judge much better than I what to can and what to keep? Did I have the option of simply destroying the private things: letters, postcards, casual confessions? Or of just heaving them out? I once knew a writer who on completion of a book would stuff a plastic bag with all versions, drafts, notes, correspondence, and so on, and drop it in the trash can. Once, on trash-collection day, he had mistakenly tossed his daughter's examination paper along with everything else and he and all of his friends, as if in a favela in South America, had to wander through the smoking heaps of the Göttingen town dump until they found not only the daughter's awful paper on Flaubert but also the writer's notes for his novel—notes that revealed beyond any doubt that he had plagiarized sentences word for word from various other authors. Anyone who has ever visited the stacks at Marbach, that gigantic index file of rampant orderliness erected on top of all those writers' messy life histories, will begin to doubt the reasonableness of preserving all that paper as an index to all that failure. The complete collected failures, now set on view for the voyeurs of literary research, who fall upon it only too eagerly, using it to pad out their tedious dissertations and articles. Why are there archives for writers, and not for the so-called simple man? Danilo Kiš, a Serb who died in Paris, one of the most moving authors of my generation, once wrote a story about an archive in Sweden that housed the life stories of all the people never mentioned in any reference work, including the story of his own unlucky father. An unforgettable story, it quietly insists that every life has a meaning, and for that reason alone must not be lost to us after death. It is one of the saddest and most beautiful stories in world literature, because it describes with great love something that does not exist and that, despite our modern mania for preserving everything, never will exist. Fifty percent of all human beings are forgotten by the second generation, and the rest are forgotten by the third. Some survive as the names of streets. The father of Danilo Kiš died in a horrific way and, except for the remembrance written by his son, nothing remains of him, not even a gravestone.

Exhausted, I leaned heavily on the tabletop with both hands, and with my thumbs tried to spread out the pile of paper. What destiny has brought you all together? I asked the pages, which had gradually begun to yield some of their secrets. An invoice for flowers sent to Germany. A note: "High-altitude flight? How often can one crash in a single lifetime? The desire for security and justice on the one hand, and for beauty on the other—this is what creates the gods. Copyright protection for ideas that were never written down, but were thought of. Who do you take yourself for? Everything depends on that. (C)[=Canetti: trans.] For those who don't believe in immortality, it doesn't exist. (B.)[=Börne: trans.] Retraining a poet to be a writer."

Then a few letters from a doctoral student in Halle, very scholarly and preachy, as if Rudolf were incapable of answering the young man's questions on his own. And, at last, a find.

It practically forced me to sit in Rudolf's chair, for this was something that had to be read with Rudolf's eyes. I forgot completely my own dictum that violating someone's private life is one of those terrible crimes we all commit on a daily basis, and fell upon the first letter of the bundle I had shaken loose from the pile. Eva's hand, no doubt about it. The strange, crabbed hand of that very Eva whom Rudolf insisted he had never seen again, whom he had not, outside of a few nasty phone conversations, heard "breathe a word" in thirty years. "Thank God"—I remembered his exact words—"because it would kill me if ever I fell into her clutches again." He had often asked me to pass along any news of the old "hens," and I had always reported back to him whatever I read about them, had even sent him newspaper clippings, which he'd made sarcastic comments about. There had been a few clippings about Eva. She had written a little book for one of those gender series that had sprung up like mushrooms, a book called *Women and Art.* Rudolf had so lambasted it with ridicule ("Females in Jails") that I, although I'd skimmed it and found its central thesis dubious, felt obliged to defend it from his damning verdict. When, later on, in my own defense and Eva's, I sent him a favorable review from our local paper, he was dumbfounded that anyone could take seriously a text so thinly argued, so poorly written, and so devoid of convincing examples; he had immediately surmised, in this rant, that the reviewer must have slept with the author. "If only she had stayed in his bed," he cried out with a contempt unusual even for him, "rather than infiltrating the university!" He had then shifted effortlessly from this anemic newspaper review to conclusions about the state of the arts in Germany as a whole, which had gone "downriver" some time ago, and the mere existence of this reviewer, a teacher of art history somewhere up north, was reason enough for him never to entertain the idea of a job offer from a German university. In German universities, thought has potentially life-threatening consequences. Illumination is avoided; learning preferably takes place in semi-darkness. Once the first flush of his excitement had passed, he fell into a lethargic and melancholy mood, which abruptly shifted to utter apathy. "Thank goodness I didn't waste any more time at German institutions of higher learning," he would say in conclusion. Of course, there had been attempts, acknowledging the publication of his novels and his growing prestige, to lure him back with a professor's chair; one was even especially endowed for him, but he always replied with impeccably formulated reasons for his grateful, polite rejection of such offers. "Where in Germany is there a terrace for my animals?" he would ask me whenever we discussed these issues on the telephone, because for him there was no case to be made for living outside Turin, in what he called Flatland. Though he never went to the cinema and in his last few years had not set foot in a theater, either (after Strehler, there was no theater in Italy worthy of the name), Rudolf could not imagine life without the ambience of a city, without movies, theaters, and restaurants. And whenever I reproached him for changing his lifestyle to that of an anchorite, he would say, "As long as I can look out from above, from my terrace, on theaters, movies, and other public institutions of culture, that is enough." But in a German-speaking country? Never. "Just think if you had to live in Paderborn," he would shout. "Podunk U.! Apartment C4, University Housing, in Podunk-Paderborn! And your neighbor in the two-family flat next door was this art historian, the guy Eva extorted that disgraceful review from, riddled through with equal parts ignorance and megalomania!"

What did he have against Paderborn? I myself preferred Paderborn and its environs to Munich or Berlin, and had been thinking that I might settle down there sometime soon. In Paderborn you can look people in the eye a little longer without getting tired; you can listen to them a little longer without getting sick of their voices. And, in any case, they don't have much to say.

I enjoyed Rudolf's brilliant, perverse telephone tantrums, but as the calls were usually on my bill I kept them short. Besides, I had no real arguments to defend Eva's theory-soaked diatribes on how everything feminine in art was muzzled. There are books we simply should take a pass on: we don't have to love them passionately or hate them extravagantly. Eva wrote the way people do when they are indifferent to public opinion but still want to be in step with the times. Most likely, she had just wanted to raise her hand, say something, be noticed. Rudolf's rabid attack had bothered me because I could not imagine that he had any interest in Eva's subject, or that after almost forty years he still cared about her. He had loved her once in a superficial way, but I never knew why, not even back in Berlin. Eva's self-indulgent passivity, her inability to make conversation, her lack of wit and verve were even then the subject of long discussions, as were her constant headaches and her sour expression after the first glass of wine, which made us ask ourselves whether we should bother to include her in our gatherings at all. But the minute we'd decide to drop her Rudolf would begin defending her and her cheerfulness and charm. She was the very opposite of those gray university girls who looked contemptuously down on everyone from their theoretical heights. Her cautiousness, her fear of risk, were signs of her contemplative strength. Within a few seconds, his overblown praises would transform her into someone entirely different from the creature his invective had made of her moments before. And so she stayed on in our kitchen, pedantic, crabby, anything but cheerful or charming.

Now, totally unguarded, I was opening the letters from Eva to Rudolf—love letters, despite their curiously dry tone. The last one, only a few weeks old, was clearly the high point of a tragic love affair. I could tell Rudolf had read it, as there were handwritten notes in the margin. "I finally spoke with Ernst," I read, "and he seems to be in agreement, if everything is resolved quickly and he can keep the house in Spain. Evidently the house means more to him than I do. Although I said, in our very quiet conversation (at least, it got quiet toward the end) that the sole reason for the split is that we don't love each other anymore, he suspects someone else in the wings. All these years I have underestimated his fundamental lack of trust. He even goes as far as to mistrust himself. Is it a man or a woman? he finally asked me, and I don't quite know whether this is his normal cynicism and his indifference to me, or he suspects something, or actually knows. I turned my desk inside out to see if one of your letters was lying around, but I couldn't find anything, and the secret compartment seemed not to have been touched."

In the next letter (one compact page composed on a typewriter, not a computer) she brought up all kinds of memories that, now that the whole process had started, she could allow herself to think about; if she had been fearful up to the point of taking the "step," she was now calm and confident. "I don't want to press you," the last paragraph began, "but I would be happy if now you dared to take the step too"—yet another step—"since it will take longer than I thought to leave my work at the university, not least because of some appraisals I have to do. In any event, I must stick it out for the winter semester (Dürer's drawings). Anything new on where we might live? If I had my way, I would prefer a house (even in the country), but if E. were to clear out voluntarily I would not object to living in your place at the institute. (You know how fond I am of animals, but I am probably not the right person to supervise the zoo. On the other hand, I am a meticulous gardener!) What I would like most, of course, would be for you to take the job at Brandeis, since there I would have the chance (which I hardly would in Italy) of finding some kind of academic position. My last three articles have now been published in America—you can be proud of me!—so I wouldn't be arriving there a tabula rasa, and if my NYU lecture in October goes well something would surely work out."

Her closing remarks I skimmed. I would have to wait till the afternoon to read them properly, for now I began to hear voices and footsteps out in the hallway—Marta and, as I soon found out, the university president's. With icy objectivity, the objectivity of the professional executor for whom the peccadilloes and erotic preferences of a deceased client are matters of complete indifference, I placed the letters back inside their gray cardboard file and returned the file to its place in the stack. When the two walked in, in good humor, they found me sitting at an empty desk, motionless, as if I had had a stroke. I had the uneasy feeling that my life was about to take a critical turn.

Chapter 9

THE HUMILIATING EXPERIENCE of reading those letters had taken away any appetite I might have had for lunch or conversation, so I tried, successfully in the end, to talk the president out of going to a restaurant; I suggested that we try a café under the arcade near the Goethe Institute, where I had once been years ago, with one of the institute's former directors. We had become friends during a very successful conference on the topic "Myth and Modernism." Klaus. An agile mind. A born planner and a great organizer.

A few weeks before, I had come across Klaus's obituary in the *Süddeutsche Zeitung,* placed there by his friends, and was annoyed not to find my own name on the list of mourners. He had committed suicide in Brazil: if the rumors were correct, on account of a woman.

Yet could I really speak of Klaus as a friend? We had seen each other perhaps five times in our lives, spoken on the phone ten times, and exchanged a dozen letters. But when we met in the café under the arcade by the Goethe Institute he had told me the story of his life. And that's what was different about Klaus. When I think about people I feel I am closer to, I usually remember just an episode—some funny or serious or ridiculous detail. But when I think about Klaus what appears before me is his whole life, which back then he had presented to me as one continuous love tragedy. I had given a talk in Turin on Bataille, at that time a favorite of the unorthodox left, and on his theory of the potlatch, or gift economy, an extravagant theory that had meant a great deal; had in fact become a key text for people fed up with the bourgeois trivialities of daily life in the West German republic. All big spenders are tightwads at heart, Klaus had said after my talk. Even Bataille, whom I had defended elaborately, was in Klaus's view just a misdirected, middle-class piker. I remembered how the wind beneath the arcades was picking up strength; suddenly, it blew over a metal newsstand—making an incredible noise—then got into the papers, riffling their pages, blowing them apart, and how the now separated leaves, freed from the burden of one another, flew in strange, flapping motions beneath the swaying lampposts. "What can you expect of a man like Bataille, who spent his whole life in a library?" asked Klaus the big spender, who was probably secretly a cheapskate himself.

I briefly narrated the story of my friend's suicide to the president, to justify my insistence on this particular café. He paid grudging attention as we walked over—it wasn't likely he had much interest in a man he didn't know, and besides, he was mourning the loss of the four-course lunch he could have written off his taxes. However, once we'd been seated in the café's wicker chairs he made the casual yet clearly embarrassed observation that I seemed to know a lot of suicides. Certainly, I answered, anyone who has intellectually lively friends will occasionally make the sad discovery that for one of them life became unbearable. The president made a concerned face, sipped the Diet Coke he'd ordered with his toasted ham sandwich, and seemed to be relieved when I explained that I would be unable to give him a more detailed survey of the literary estate before the end of the week. "I understand, of course, call me anytime," he said, and mentioned his fervent hope that he could soon read the fragmentary *Testament*. "Aren't most twentieth-century German novels fragments," he exclaimed. "Kafka, Musil?" Then he snapped his carefully manicured fingers—to no effect, it turned out—at the waiter, saying he could not be late for a meeting he had called. "We'll see each other at the memorial service for Rudolfo," he shouted back at me as he headed off. "I'll have an invitation sent to you."

I let him go, happy to have a moment alone to think about Klaus. We met for the last time in Munich, where he had been on an assignment at the headquarters of the Goethe Institute. He was suffering from a bad cold, and I was recovering from a bout of sciatica. But, despite our poor health, we drove out to a little village near Erding, where Klaus insisted on visiting a pilgrimage church, Maria Thalheim, because a friend of his ("believe it or not") had once been cured there. I forget what the illness was. But I can still see the costly votive gifts in that church—little carved human figures, some displaying stunning craftsmanship.

Klaus didn't want to leave, so impressed was he by this Bavarian piety. And even I, bent over with pain, enjoyed spending time near the image of the Blessed Virgin, if only to exhibit to her my suffering. We sat down on a bench in front of an elderberry bush (the reason for the pilgrimages: every year the bush bore berries, but it never bloomed first) and Klaus told me of his latest unhappy love affair, with one of Rudolf's assistants, a woman who would not be going with him to his next Goethe Institute assignment. Marta? I wondered. Had it been Marta? Certainly he had told me the woman's name as we sat by the miraculous elderberry bush, but I couldn't remember it now. Rudolf had always kept his distance from Klaus. "A man of taste," Rudolf would say, "but not my kind of guy," and never accepted Klaus's often repeated invitation to come and speak at the Goethe Institute in Turin.

A deep sadness had descended upon me, a depression that, like a kind of sponge, threatened to sop up my own will to live.

At the next table, some Japanese students were reading to one another from the menu, laughing out loud while making odd, convulsive gestures, as if they had one of the funniest texts in Europe before them. They all had sweet, innocent faces. Interesting to imagine the outcome if one of the great Italian masters had seen them. Since the president had neglected to pay his bill (and mine), and since I couldn't make the case to the waiter that I didn't know the well-dressed man who'd shared my table, I had to pay for both of us. For a while I stood by the Goethe Institute sign, trying to remember the last words Klaus had spoken to me, but I soon gave up, foiled by the racket from the crowd that had just rushed in under the arcade to get out of a light rain. I thrust my hands deep in my pockets and started walking back to work.

It was an effort, but I forced myself to think about Eva, to visualize what I had been reading. As I walked through the growing crowd of people, jostling their shopping bags and briefcases and packages, after a while I was able to bring her into focus—her face, a few of her characteristic gestures, her walk, her laughter (rare though it was), the way she used to arch her eyebrows and turn down the left corner of her mouth. All at once several images of her flickered through my brain: at our kitchen table; on Lake Wannsee, where we used to go for long outings in a two-seated paddleboat; at the gallery Haus am Wannsee, with the painter Fred Thieler and the gallery owner Manfred de la Motte ("Smile, now, and I'll give you a cookie," he had said to Eva, who had glared at him); in the Dahlem Museums with the old masters; at the Vaganten-Bühne Theater on Kantstrasse, where I was an extra, performing with the great Peter Herzog. And as I made my way through the throng, turning these images over in my mind, others popped up like Polaroid pictures that I had forgotten—or else was imagining now: Eva and me in Rome—in the Villa Borghese, outside the little movie theater on the Campo dei Fiori, engrossed in a poster from one of Truffaut's films—and I suddenly recalled that, on one of her excursions to the Eternal City, she had paid me a short visit (two days and one brief night) while I was working for six weeks as a visiting auditor in the cultural department of the German Embassy. When had that been, exactly? Maybe thirty years ago? Winter, in any case. We stood freezing outside a bar on a little square behind the Piazza Navona, drinking beer, when suddenly, from out of the darkness, a group of her girlfriends converged on us. Now she had to decide. I can still see myself at the bar (Bar Paradiso?), Eva talking with her friends, but I have forgotten what it was that prompted her to come away with me. Baroque Rome in the winter rain: that was what I had to offer her. We probably talked the whole time about Rudolf, and Caravaggio, but now, in the Turin rain, I could not remember what we'd said.

I took some detours through lesser-known neighborhoods, so as not to get back to my desk too quickly. Although I actually wanted to get to the river, to the Basilica di Superga, I ended up at the Santuario della Consolata and had to go all the way back down the Corso Regina Margherita. I had lost all sense of direction. I was utterly disoriented—people and places seemed to be dancing, rocking, and spinning till I grew dizzy.

I had to figure out how it was that Eva's and Rudolf's paths had crossed again, and how from this coincidence—or maybe it had been no coincidence—a lasting relationship had resulted, a lifelong one, to judge from Eva's letter; at any rate, the kind of relationship that Eva and I, despite all her efforts, at least, had not been able to establish. I wondered: perhaps the failure of our love affair—in reality an affair of miscommunication—had been the necessary precondition for Eva and Rudolf's finding each other again. Perhaps I had served, without knowing it, as the bridge between them.

As the rain threatened to turn into a real downpour, I took refuge in a bar near the Mole Antonelliana. In spite of the multitude of espresso drinkers milling about, I found an empty table and sat down with my notebook. I felt an urgent need to write, but nothing came to mind except sentimental memories. I drank a few Cynars, which inspired me to draw a ghostly sketch of Eva. It was not a pretty picture. A sixty-year-old woman using whatever weapons she had left to seduce the sixty-year-old Rudolf so they could spend their twilight years together. A woman who felt not even the slightest twinge of objective sympathy for Elsa. Elsa, who had made Rudolf's self-indulgent asceticism possible in the first place, should just "clear out." A sense of the monstrousness of Eva's letter was sprouting in me—a poisonous seedling, and to rid myself of it I deleted my sketch with violent strokes of the pen.

As I threw myself into this act of righteous vandalism, I felt sure that I was being watched. A young man who was standing at the now nearly empty bar had apparently thought my sketch rather good, and as I looked up he sat down at my table, uninvited, glass in hand. A German who spoke German or, rather, whispered it: "Are you a painter or a writer, or both?" Both, I told him. And he proceeded, then and there, to present me with his opinion of Germany.

"The state is the enemy of capital," he rasped, with irritation, as though I had claimed the opposite. He was a representative for Fiat in Germany, which apparently gave him the right to annoy his compatriots in Italy. "If Rudolf had known you," I said right to his baffled face, "he would have had a real reason for killing himself."

Chapter 10

AT THE INSTITUTE, ALL WAS DARK. Feeling like a burglar, I managed with great effort to unlock the heavy front door, cracking it open just wide enough to squeeze through with my overnight bag. Had anyone spotted me? I envisioned a police patrol, suspicions aroused, pistols drawn and safety catches off, escorting me at gunpoint into the building. Maybe I should have stayed in a hotel after all. I had now been two days in this city, and nothing had gone easily or naturally. Surprises lurked everywhere, yet every encounter was like a prearranged move in a game of chess. The one constant throughout my stay in Turin had been my grief, laid out rigidly over the fluid folds of inconsistencies and confusion.

Even the baggage check in the railroad station had nearly bested me. I was informed that my bag could not be found. The official in charge had repeatedly come back to the counter, shrugging, holding up his palms. "Are you *sure* you left your suitcase here?" he asked me again and again. And each time, with increasing precision, I made clear to him that we were not dealing with a suitcase but with an overnight bag—*un sacco,* a bag, do you understand?—which I had indeed left at this very counter, as my claim stub proved beyond any doubt. To bring our fruitless discussion to an end, I could have made off with any one of several lovely suitcases without the least opposition from anyone—and with the vigorous support of the cab driver, who was in a hurry to get home for dinner. "Nice. That one," he said, as the sweating official heaved a huge red Samsonite suitcase onto the counter and offered to grab the monster by its grip and stow it for me. Funny, what people will try to palm off on you when your own things are missing. Our luggage master would have let us simply walk off with it, and later he would have tried, as he was now doing with me, to force a blue suitcase, also a Samsonite, onto the owner of the red one. The crowning accomplishment of his career would be to have everyone en route to anywhere via Turin running around in someone else's clothing.

It was not until a higher official arrived on the scene, and ordered a complete search of the entire luggage inventory, that matters were concluded with the wished-for result. "Oh, a *bag,*" the friendly counterman murmured with relief. "I thought you were looking for a *suitcase.*" When the supervisor started to make disparaging remarks about his bag-checker, in an effort to apologize for the incompetence of his ill-trained subordinates, I gave the man an ostentatiously big tip for his efforts, which he pocketed without a word of thanks. The two were probably in cahoots.

I crept noiselessly up to the apartment, remembering how Rudolf had always described his own homecomings. When he got back from his travels, worn out and depressed, he liked to "effect silent reentry." Sometimes he would go straight to the station restaurant, ensuring that he wouldn't run into anyone at the institute waiting to welcome him back. He didn't want to be welcomed, and he didn't want to be asked how his trip had gone. The very idea of Elsa heading him off at the apartment door and giving him that "concerned" look, he told me on the phone, was reason enough to go to the office first thing. There he would drop his coat and bag and then, casually, as if by accident, turn up in the apartment. He didn't bother with explanations. But I could never understand, given this attitude, how he successfully managed his official life as director of the institute, for this kind of hugger-mugger was in no way consistent with the strict traditions of the university. "That gang of ghastly bureaucrats," he would say, allowing of no exceptions. "Worse than the Germans."

He often telephoned me while he was on the road, preferably after midnight, when he couldn't sleep in whatever sleazy hotel he was staying. Another one of his odd quirks. The better off he was financially, the worse were the hotels he chose. The fleabags near the train station were his favorites, with "remnants"—his word—as his fellow guests. "Remnants with life stories—life stories as remnants," he'd say. He collected the stories, the oral histories of the people who occupy the worn-out plastic armchairs in the cramped lobbies of cheap hotels. Long before the events of 1989, he met a constant stream of Georgians, Belarusians, Chechens, and Chuvashes, who had somehow, God knows by what underground railroad, found their way west: gentlemen with lots of gold teeth who recounted their odysseys at extravagant length and in extraordinary detail—fantastic ballads of poverty, filled with grief and pain and picaresque adventures. Rudolf had even contemplated publishing these stories, which he preserved in notebooks, but the idea got no further than a statement in an interview. In his opinion there was no other literature that spanned with such immediacy the most significant and the least significant, the highest and the lowest, the most important and the least important material of the twentieth century. This was the true epic of modernism. It was only because our intellect had been compromised and, in a deeper sense, anesthetized that we didn't take sufficient account of the stories of Eastern Europe, which he termed the last European stories, period. "Or would you describe *your* life as worth writing about?" a rhetorical question to which, thank God, he never expected an answer.

I had often asked myself whether Rudolf's predilection for single-room-occupancy hotels had anything to do with his background, which he was careful to keep in the dark. "It is not anyone's business where I come from, what my parents' names were, or whether I knew them or not," he would say when asked about his childhood. He loved to make a mystery of himself. While his colleagues wasted their energies on literary festivals, he sat in cheap hotels and listened to stories. And whenever he called me at night he would tell me that I was not to reveal his whereabouts to anyone, especially Elsa, who under no circumstances was to know how to get hold of him. Sometimes he even begged me to call her and ask for him at home, so that I could reassure him afterward that she didn't know where he was. This weird stealthiness became more pronounced right after his first novel was published, when the publisher sent him on an extended reading tour of Germany, made possible by a doctor friend who wrote him a medical certificate affirming that he had a serious illness and must be relieved of all teaching obligations. So, for the first time in his life, he started going to places like Göttingen, Wolfsburg, and Husum; he stayed overnight in Lüneburg, where he gave a reading at the Heine House. It was in Lüneburg that his nocturnal phone calls began; he later confessed to me that these had more than once saved his life. Although he eagerly embraced the rigors of these reading tours, which followed every new publication, they inevitably hurtled him into frigid depths of total depression, which I would then patiently have to analyze with him. Towns, people, meetings, coincidences—all were potential catalysts for his darkest thoughts, and we would go over every detail. The question that always ended these conversations was, How can you exist in this Germany, in this middle-class lie, this wasteland?

Since things on the whole were going well for me, and since, despite all our criticism of our country's native provinciality, I was inclined to defend Germany's attempt to support a viable cultural life, on more than one occasion, toward the end of these nocturnal seances, Rudolf would begin abusing me, as if I, rather than these German towns and their awful hotels, were to blame for the misery that assaulted him. It was as if I personally had designed the ugly fountains and ordered the construction of the pedestrian malls, had chopped down trees that before the war had stood on the squares in front of the hotels, as he knew from old postcards. Once I made a special trip to Lüneburg to keep him from jumping off the church steeple—in emulation of the engineer who had leaped to his death because the steeple was out of plumb. In two days I was able to revive his interest in living again. "You have to have the courage not to be *final* about anything," I told him, and these words brought him back to life, even to laughter. I never enjoyed myself more than when walking with him through these odd cities, roaring with laughter at the hopeless, absurd state of modern architecture. Nothing was more fun than the two of us ridiculing the cuisine served in the self-styled good, old-fashioned restaurants. But then again nothing was sadder for me than seeing him standing on the railway platform with shoulders stooped, one hand raised awkwardly, as if hung with weights, in a halfhearted goodbye as my train pulled out. The pure joy of a minute before would give way in an instant to bitter despondency. I knew then he would call me that very night, his dry, hoarse voice bemoaning the pointlessness of having traveled to whatever ruined city he happened to find himself in. But somehow he always managed to get through all the readings and the question-and-answer sessions, and after four weeks, drained and slack, he would noiselessly return and thread himself back into his daily routine, as though he had never been away at all.

Thanks! You saved my life. I had several postcards with this laconic message.

Silently, I climbed the stairs to his apartment, as if by imitating Rudolf I could feel something of the emotional burdens he had brought home after those excursions to Germany. Until now I'd been convinced that for the past few years he had cut off all links with his homeland, but after seeing Eva's letters I had my doubts. And Brandeis? Eva had written that she would have liked to see him take the job at Brandeis; her motive for this was transparent. Eva could hardly speak Italian, and hadn't the discipline to learn it now. Besides, Italians probably didn't have much use for gender theories applied to art history. Her studies are a gender unto themselves, Rudolf used to say. Nothing but derision and mockery, never a good word for the woman. And yet now, a few stair treads away, was a thick wad of letters that turned everything I thought I knew about Rudolf and Eva on its head.

I hadn't come to Turin to shed light on the immediate reasons for Rudolf's suicide, but I was beginning to feel an obligation—resist it though I might—to worry about those reasons, and, like a detective, to look into his death itself. In this house my friend had taken his own life; barely two weeks ago he had stood on these stairs and considered the manner in which he would end it. Had he talked about it with Elsa, with Marta—or with Eva?

———

I was quite certain that I had locked the apartment door when I left, but it opened as soon as I turned the latch. I had to smile when I saw the name plate: a visiting card dating back to our Berlin days. The address had been crossed out with pencil but was still clearly legible. It had been my own last address in the city: 4 Ahornstrasse, Berlin-Zehlendorf. For reasons I have forgotten, Rudolf had ordered visiting cards printed right after he received his fellowship, and he gave them out lavishly at first. None of his friends—least of all me—possessed such a thing as a visiting card; we considered them the worst kind of Babbittry. He, on the other hand, really wanted to see his name embossed on these little white squares, as if this gave them a deeper meaning somehow; he would feel the raised letters with his thumb whenever he handed one of them out.

There was light coming from one of the rooms, casting a faint quadrangle-shaped glow out into the corridor. A peaceful light, less for work than for meditation. Someone in there was waiting for me, and even before I reached the door I heard a whimpering sound, which trailed off into a sigh. It was Marta, sitting slumped at my workstation, crying. Her elbows were propped on the table, her head in her hands—a classic pose. I lingered in the doorway, still in my overcoat and holding my bag; I was unsure whether to interpret her presence and her state of mind as interference, as an infringement on my territory—for there were certainly other places in this city where she could give vent to her grief. She should not be in the apartment, and she most certainly should not be letting herself go on like this in front of me. But what irritated me most was the timid, anxious way she stared at me, for up to now her lack of fear had been a defining characteristic—that absence of even the slightest shyness or reticence in her makeup. Now, with Elsa confined to hospital, my unpleasant first impression of Marta might soon expand to define my entire view of her. She was behaving as if she, not Elsa, were the widow. Was she married? I tried to recall our conversation of the previous evening, but not much of it had stayed with me. Now here she was, tear-soaked and wretched, the very picture of misery. Rudolf's death was old news; this great a change must have some other explanation.

"What's happened?" I asked.

My sudden appearance must have made it clear to her that she had gone well beyond her self-set limits. She immediately took her hands from her face, sat up straight as a ramrod, and said in a gentler than usual tone, "Caesar is dead."

I cannot say what it was about this image of a grief-stricken woman that moved me so, but I could feel tears welling up in my eyes. Caesar was dead, and that was bad enough—a tragedy, in fact, since quite obviously the reason for it was Rudolf's absence, or, rather, the absence of his affection. Rudolf had loved this ugly dog, this infinitely unattractive creature, this mockery of even the most far-fetched concept of beauty. In his old age, Caesar had become so gracelessly unlovely that even the most sympathetic outsider would have been unable to see the slightest trace of the perfection that had once—perhaps—been his. A slobbering wreck of an animal. But Rudolf had never concluded a phone call without telling me how Caesar was and mentioning the touching devotion with which his pet would rise to greet him when he walked onto the roof terrace. All humankind had been put on earth for the sole purpose of disturbing Rudolf and obstructing his work: Caesar was the one creature who helped him keep going. They understood each other. Rudolf was firmly convinced of this, and one of his best short stories was written as a conversation with a dog—and it was dedicated to Caesar. I recalled how Rudolf once suggested that I collaborate with him on an anthology of stories about talking dogs; so I was always sending him texts of this sort, from Svevo to Flaiano, which he collected in a special file. "You do the animals, I will write the afterword," he said. But the dog anthology never got any further than a file; neither did the collection of writings on moles—from Pliny through Hegel and up to the present—that he had planned with his Berlin friends Wolf Lepenies and Henning Ritter. Rudolf hardly ever threw anything away; both files must still be here: my dog stories and his mole dossier. Now Caesar was dead.

Something had happened indeed.

I put my bag down, took off my coat, and went over to Marta and put my arms around her. We had said nothing except "What's happened?" and "Caesar is dead." She not only permitted my embrace but embraced me in turn with a neediness that made me even sadder. There we stood, a pair of survivors, weeping at my desk. Marta had spread out photographs of Rudolf and Caesar, pictures of two departed friends; waves of sadness washed over us. Just giving ourselves up to the pain was a relief. At last, something that had been dammed up inside me since the news of Rudolf's death took form, began flowing out. My earlier state of mind, vacillating between misery and mutiny, had yielded to a pliant tenderness that left no room for rigidity or toughness, and even my body seemed to have no bones.

After some time, with an effort, we managed to separate. It was already past ten o'clock, and I wanted to, had to, get to work; not even Caesar's death was going to keep me from uncovering the mystery concealed within those gray file boxes. But since Marta, looking dazed and rumpled after our long embrace, once more stood before me in the role of the widow, I could not keep from asking her brutally—no more beating around the bush—about Eva's role in the household. I should never have brought it up.

"Eva? A whore who ruined our lives."

"Our?"

No direct answer. Instead, I got a rambling rant that no amount of patient listening could put in order. But even chaos that is consistent can be form of a kind, and I got the impression that Marta, with her stops and starts, her emotional outbursts and exaggerated gesticulations, was deliberately using a rhetoric of disorganization to pull the wool over my eyes. A widow who would not admit to being one was talking about another widow who clearly had more right to feel that she was one, while the legal widow lay possibly dying. I couldn't tell exactly what she was driving at, her speech was so disjointed. One thing was clear: Marta's unhealthy hatred had been pent up too long. At last she was loosing her storm cloud, hurling her thunderbolts. But to give her rage at least a semblance of objectivity she accused Eva of being the real reason that Rudolf had never completed his novel. Her restlessness, her emotional tyranny, her hysterical phone calls—to say nothing of her relentless criticism of completed portions of Rudolf's book, which Rudolf himself had called only fragments, or sketches—had always thrown him right back to Point Zero. She had in her office downstairs, she said, all the pages Eva had savaged in red pencil and sent back to Rudolf, and from these one could see without a doubt that Eva hadn't had the faintest idea of the structure or the significance of the work.

I decided not to inquire how she could make such a serious accusation, given her inadequate German; initiating any intelligent discussion after her outburst seemed pointless. What bothered me more was the obvious truth that Eva had played some kind of a role in Rudolf's life, and, quite possibly, in his death.

At this point I was so absorbed in my gathering suspicions that I had forgotten Marta completely. Now, as if she had cried herself into a state of complete vulnerability, she began taking off her clothes and dropping them on the floor. Then she crawled into the bed and pulled the coverlet up to her forehead, so that only a Medusan wreath of hair on the pillow attested to her presence. Through all of this she said not a word. From beneath the covers came an occasional long, muffled sigh, followed before long by the sound of regular breathing. To spare her, after the shock she had doubtless suffered at Caesar's death, I carefully picked the carton of Eva's letters off the stack and slipped into the kitchen, to swim alone in my whirlpool of uncertainties.

Eva's letters were still on top; Marta had done no snooping in my absence. I wondered why Rudolf, who before his death had personally filled these gray boxes, and left them as his literary estate—hadn't thrown Eva's letters away. No matter what their relationship had been—my guess was an especially nasty form of co-dependency—it was nobody's business. But had Eva also become an integral part of his work, a chapter, a theme? Had he deliberately *not* thrown out this epistolary trash because he was determined that it should one day be exposed?

Dearest, the letters began, and then came thanks for Rudolf's letters, which clearly had been sent every few days. He must have provided her with minute descriptions of his daily life, of his misery, for, in her pedantic and small-minded way, Eva had responded to all of it: problems with the university; Elsa; his writing; the animals; politics. Often her letters read like a teacher's evaluation in an elementary-school report card: well behaved, occasionally sleeps in class; sometimes stirs up trouble; all in all a good boy who won't go terribly far, but far enough. Page after page. And then I read the following: "Perhaps you should get rid of

Caesar," she wrote him, "because if he dies in your presence you will never be able to get it behind you." Get it behind you! As I read these letters, I felt my curiosity turn to hate. Hate is the loneliest emotion: the stronger it became, the more lost I felt. How dared Eva give Rudolf such abysmal advice? In her prim, know-it-all manner. And never the least doubt of the rightness of her judgment, never a hint of modesty, never a flicker of fear. She must have been completely sure of her role in his life.

The longer I read, the more nauseated I became. If I was correctly interpreting what he had written himself from its echo in Eva's letters, Rudolf, the great poet of descent and farewell, either must have been playing a nasty trick, fashioning himself a theater of illusions, to shore up his fading magic, or had been so desperate to escape the growing sadness of his later years that he had picked Eva as an anchor to windward. There was much to be said for the first theory. Increasingly, Rudolf had become a joyless gambler, resorting to all sorts of new tricks to outsmart the fate that had dealt him a losing hand, to beat the impossible odds against his being able to complete his *Testament*. On the phone to me at midnight, he spoke of the graveyard of words expanding around him. "God knows, not Gray's country churchyard all ordered and tidy, but a completely ordinary, ugly modern cemetery littered with everyday, worn-out, corrupted words, a boneyard of trivialities," he would say. "Only a con man or a fool would want to cobble something together out of this rubbish." "And so, given that insight, what are you up to now?" I asked. "I'm asking for a reprieve," Rudolf had answered—one of those little phrases he always used, and which he always followed with a snarky laugh.

It was well past midnight. For too long I had been palpating the letters for those artificial emotional tremors that Eva would set up for Rudolf to hear. Ardently, she would open up the ledger of her shortcomings for him, so that three days later she would hear from him that he still loved her in spite of it all; her self-denigrating confessions, aimed at getting him to stoop to her level, revolted me so profoundly that when I finally came across her first reference to me I didn't recognize it. But it was me she was talking about, all right, and I was clearly a problem. She did not quite know, she wrote, exactly how she should handle this problem (me): "To get back at me, he will probably side with Elsa. And of course he will see our relationship as an attack on your friendship with him. All the same, he has been following me around for years with his tongue hanging out, and if I had even once given him encouragement I would have been stuck with him for the rest of my life, as you have been. A long time ago, during the year he spent in Rome, he begged me (in tears!) in his clumsy, unmanly way to stay with him, and because it was freezing cold that winter I came within a hair's breadth of giving in. His helplessness did awaken my maternal feelings, but even then, thank God, I was strong enough not to fall for his line. You must tell him! And you must be clear to leave him nothing to say. As you know, I am convinced that his false enthusiasm is extremely harmful to you."

Rudolf had penciled in a little question mark in the margin—that was something, at least: a fragile, shy little question mark to stand up against those disgraceful accusations, those howling absurdities that, sentence by sentence, were meant to undermine our friendship. The letter went on and on. Even Rudolf must have sensed that an unconscionable attempt was being made to disenfranchise him, for on the following pages, where the portrait of me was completed in the nastiest way, the strike-throughs, exclamation points, and question marks grew more and more frequent; at one point, where Eva went completely off the rails, with the craziest speculations on my bad character, he had noted in the margin "hysterical old cow." As for me, I was sickened by her arrogance, which was based on nothing but the meanness of her basic nature, and especially by her traitorous attempt to shove me out of his life. Rudolf had evidently written a response to this attempted character assassination, but a timid one, tentatively argued, for she had been bold enough to slap it down in her next letter: how could he be taken in by my pitiful maneuvers, by my "clownish masquerade," which was meant only to flatter him and secure my place as a court jester in the palace of his imagination. A ridiculous waste of energy, she wrote, for Rudolf to put up with me any longer. For the sake of the years they had shared, now was the time to make a clean break of it, "to cast off the chains he has put on you" in order to find the peace and equanimity to finish his work. If I continued as the "moral supervisor" of his work, Rudolf could abandon forever any idea of completing his book.

There was no way that I could read the whole bundle of these insulting documents, yet the invective they contained kept pulling me back with an irresistible force, as if some truth were hidden in them, however annihilating that truth might be. It was pathetic. A few times I was tempted to call Eva up and confront her directly, but I knew I was too drained to ask the necessary questions calmly. My stock of ability to judge was almost depleted, and I had no interest in understanding or explaining anything to myself, let alone to her.

It was a relief when Marta suddenly appeared in the doorway, semi-somnolent, grief-ridden, looking like a martyred saint, and said, "Give it up." Give it up: the phrase chilled me. I rose from my chair, dazed, tossed the letters back into the carton, and followed her through the darkened apartment back to my room.

Chapter 11

I WAS MAKING HEADWAY with my work, or at least I thought I was. It even provided me with some brief flashes of pleasure, when at the end of a passage of pointless rubbish I would be rewarded with an unhoped-for "find." And I enjoyed my solitude, even if, as I secretly had to admit, it wasn't healthy.

Early that morning, after Marta had finally climbed out of bed, we went up to the terrace and wrapped Caesar in a blue silk bedspread, one of Rudolf's favorites. The chickens warily avoided us, watching with their heads cocked to one side as we dragged the corpse to the door and left it inside the apartment. I wondered who would now be monarch of this aerial Arcadia, at least until its final dissolution. The rooster clearly thought he had the inside track. But how can a rooster or a dwarf rabbit be a king? Not enough mass, too many feathers, and too much fur. Can you imagine a tortoise on a throne? In fact, yes—there is no underling who can flatter him, and he has been around too long for the lackeys to get very far with him, either.

As we were having breakfast, two responsible-looking gentlemen from the pound arrived and studied the silk spread suspiciously. I had to unroll the costly fabric—first untying the various colored ribbons Marta had used to secure it, and allow the evidence of their own eyes to convince them that it contained a dead animal. Otherwise, you might be trying to pull something over on us, their reasoning went, and in any case they were not clairvoyant. On the contrary, their job required an utter lack of sympathetic insight, the ability to remain unmoved in the presence of death. We took one last look at Caesar, then, with an effort—even in death poor Caesar had the unfortunate habit of making himself heavier than necessary—the two officials shouldered the corpse and managed to get it down the main staircase. A few students, who at this early hour had nothing better to do than smoke and chat in the hall, stared, amazed, at the strange procession. Somebody else died at the institute? they seemed to be wondering. Clearly they were studying in a charnel house. So when would it hit them? I made myself a bet that the silk bedspread, after a brief stopoff at the cleaner's today, would be draping one of the pound officials' beds, but I kept my mouth shut. Poor old Caesar. With a muffled thump he landed in the trunk of the van, and Marta paid the bill. I slipped the driver a few euros, and then, with their sad cargo, they drove off.

Marta went to her office. I was in an odd state as I ascended the stairs to the apartment again and prepared to get back to work. I had stealthily removed Eva's letters from the heap of documents and stashed them in my overnight bag, underneath my shirts. God forbid they should ever wind up in some archive. Better that the episode be expunged from Rudolf's life—I owed our friendship that much. I was thankful that my bag came equipped with a good, sturdy lock, for I was certain that when my back was turned Marta would go through my luggage. When I stopped to think about the strangeness of my actions, and the ease with which I had begun to rewrite my late friend's life, horror swept over me like an avalanche. But this feeling quickly faded; soon enough, the sangfroid of the art faker returned.

After skimming them briefly, I laid the rest of the papers back in the carton, although there were other documents among them that contained revelations of Rudolf's darker side. By what logic had he decided that they, along with Eva's letters, were to be included in his literary estate? From them I learned for the first time that Rudolf, writing under an Italian pseudonym (Ettore Totti) had produced not only feature articles about Italy but also two radio plays, which were still being run. He had also written letters to the chief editor of Southwest German Radio imploring him not to reveal Totti's true identity; rather than be known as the author of these plays, he would give up the broadcast along with the honorarium: "You surely understand, I can quite happily do without fame and fortune, as long as my anonymity is preserved." (In previous letters he had made fun of this meager honorarium and had complained, with an apt citation from Gottfried Benn's "Summa Summarum," that radio, the freelance writer's one last dependable source of income, was now leaving him in the lurch. I carefully made note of the titles of the plays and of the odd names of their alleged translators, which also smelled to me like pseudonyms, because I was certain they would lead me to a whole network of underground work. Those two plays were just the beginning.

Had Rudolf's devouring need to write been the result of an inability to leave words alone?

Even stranger was the case of his pieces—forty-seven in all—for the Bavarian Radio network, all of them broadcast under the name Giuseppe Schulz. They amounted to an entire book on Italy, surely one of the most critical ever written. Why had Rudolf, who always complained that he had no time, subjected himself to the torture of composing fifteen pages about the complex Italian political party system? By the time I had finished reading his correspondence with the Bavarian station, the reason was clear enough: he needed the money. Each honorarium was to be deposited, "as always," into "the Regensburg account." Why Regensburg? Either Rudolf had wanted to hide the money from the tax people, which seemed naive to me, or he'd wanted to hide it from Elsa, which seemed more likely. I had never had any additional source of income myself and had little notion of how such things affected one's income tax. As for Regensburg . . . I knew that Rudolf had occasionally given readings there, and that he had had only good things to say about the town, especially its antiquarian book dealers, but I could not imagine that it possessed a bookstore of such distinction and expensiveness that Rudolf would have needed a separate bank account there. I closed the carton and stuck a note on it indicating its contents. If Rudolf had really filled these boxes himself—out of character as this seemed—he must have intended to gather all his secrets in one place. But why? Had he really wanted posterity to find him out? Why hadn't he simply burned Eva's letters and instructed the savings bank in Regensburg to deposit the money into Elsa's—or Marta's—account? If, as Elsa maintained, he had asked her to appoint me as literary executor in the event of his sudden death, then he must have wanted me, at least, to know about his double life. He had wanted me to learn of Eva's treacherous attacks. What consequences had he envisioned? Was I supposed to write his biography?

The next box contained several portfolios with notes and sketches for his second novel, all on scraps of paper, in the margins of newspapers, even on the backs of papers written by his students, who were probably still waiting for their essays to be returned. I recognized the texts immediately; it would be a simple matter to match them with chapters of the published novel, particularly since the carton also contained both the original manuscript and the first typewritten version, which was scribbled over with changes. There had to be another box with the second draft, and also the printer's copy, for I knew from Rudolf that he had created four separate drafts of each of his novels and, much to the regret of his publishers, had always gone over both galleys and page proofs, making final corrections, so that for each of his slim books there existed some thousand variorum pages, each set considerably different from the others. A thrilling assignment for students, surely, to lay all these pages alongside each other and work up a comparative study: "The Genesis of a Novel."

Another find, which interested me even more, and puzzled me as well, was a cheap notebook with a blue cardboard cover on which Rudolf had written "Sources" with a felt-tipped pen. It had alphabetical tabs but was not an address book; it had probably been made in Taiwan, but not by Herlitz, whose products Rudolf usually preferred. He had often called me up with an urgent request for more Herlitz notebooks, green ones and red ones, because he was afraid his supply might run out after one of his compulsive bouts of writing. He used the red notebooks for his plots, the green ones for other ideas. Concerned that at some point one of the two colors might temporarily be unavailable, I had set up a little reserve supply at home, which I replenished as needed. There were years when he would fill as many as fifty Herlitz notebooks with his tiny script. "My memory" was his only comment. In fact, it had often happened that in the middle of a phone conversation he would put down the receiver and run to check up on a particular statement in his notes. "I can tell you exactly what you said back then—my 'memory' never fails me," he would shout triumphantly into the mouthpiece when he had found the place.

The blue "Source" was not part of this collection, which he had sometimes referred to as the Herlitz-Index.

It contained nothing by Rudolf himself; instead, it was filled with quotations, alphabetically ordered: from Adorno and Alain to Bachelard, Benn, and Blanchot; from Céline, Chateaubriand, and Cioran all the way to Zénon, Ziolkowski, and Zürn. The source for each citation was meticulously noted, and with those he had translated himself, such as Bachelard's, the original was also included. Odd, I thought: why had he not arranged the citations by theme instead?

It was now noon. My discoveries had disturbed me but not my appetite. A search of the kitchen turned up nothing more edible than a stale croissant and some rice, and I was just about to leave when Marta, with her usual telepathic talent, burst into the apartment, looking like a police detective on a security check. She gave me a fleeting hug, then, almost as casually and quickly, looked through the contents of the box on my desk. Later, I was convinced, she would send student myrmidons to search it more thoroughly. Thank goodness the mysterious blue notebook was safe in my jacket pocket.

She had brought up the mail, and now put the letters from Germany on the desk (she would answer the Italian ones herself, she said; presumably this included any to Elsa). She then sat down in the chair at the window and began manicuring her fingernails with her teeth. I had noticed during the night how she ground her teeth in her sleep, as if trying to pulverize her dreams in a pestle. At one point I had clapped my hand over her mouth, which produced a gurgling rattle followed by a period of silence. Now it was time for the claws. Tooth and claw. Not in the least bothered by my presence, she quietly gnawed and nibbled at her fingers, and on tearing loose a sliver of cuticle she pursed her lips and spat it nonchalantly onto the floor. Then she inspected her work, softened up the next finger by sucking on it, and carried on her delicate shredding operation, until all ten nails were shaped the way she wanted them shaped. A quick wipe on her pale pink blouse, one last inspection—mission accomplished! But where had she got this blouse? The night before she had been wearing a navy blue shirt, on which the tears she had been shedding over Caesar had formed dark stains. Did she live around the corner, or did she keep a closet in her office?

"Shall we get something to eat?" she asked.

For one thing, an official dinner was scheduled for a few invited guests around nine that evening, following Rudolf's memorial service, and for another there was nothing in the world I wanted less at that point than Marta's company. So I said, "I'm not hungry, I have to keep working." Laughing, she answered, "You *are* hungry, I can see it. But go ahead and starve yourself to death, if that's what you want."

An offer from Marta was not rejected with impunity.

"Are you taking me to the dinner after the service?" she asked, expectantly now, and I began looking through the mail for the invitation, which had been specifically, and correctly, directed only to me, at Rudolf's office. Since she had already opened it for me, she had to know that I could not simply show up with her in tow.

"You're so petty bourgeois, as Rudolf would have said. He would have called the president's office immediately and got me invited. How will you possibly carry on a conversation with the women there? They talk only about the university and its problems. I can come as your interpreter if we can't think of a better reason."

"Marta," I said, "there are many fine reasons to go out to dinner with you, but on this occasion I can't take you along."

I felt that I was weakening, though, and knew intuitively that after the memorial service she would grab my arm. But right now I wanted to get rid of her, to check out an idea that had jumped out at me while I was hastily thumbing through Rudolf's "Sources." As a start, I took off the jacket I had just put on and folded it carefully, so that the blue notebook wouldn't show.

"Why are you folding your jacket up like that?" said Marta. "You'll get it all wrinkled."

And since it was the only jacket I had packed for my Turin tragedy, which under Marta's clever direction was rapidly turning into a comedy, I unfolded it and put it back on. It had got me through the funeral, and now it was going to get me through the memorial service, though it really wasn't right for either event.

"Satisfied?" I asked.

Marta apparently saw that for now she had to pull in her horns and made ready to go out again, but she looked anything but satisfied.

"You Germans," she said, and slammed the heavy door behind her.

And yet she had got what she wanted. In other words, all I could think of now was her and her bullying. What more did she want from me? What did she hope to achieve—or to prevent—with her aggressive intimacy? In a few days I would be gone, at best able to resolve unanswered questions only through sporadic correspondence or telephone calls—and even that was unlikely. Once Rudolf's literary estate was housed in a German institution, German scholars trained in literary executorship would take over: experts who would be only too pleased to ignore whatever dubious information friends might supply. Authentic sources were downright taboo, and belonged at most in the gossip section of the paper, certainly not in the archive. Maybe some scholar would want my opinion on matters relating to the publication of my own correspondence with Rudolf, but that would be years from now. So what did Marta fear? Was there something in those gray boxes about her that she either wanted destroyed or interpreted in a special light? Had she had an affair with Rudolf, and did this affair have anything to do with his death? These three widows—Marta, Eva, and Elsa—stood around Rudolf's body like a gray chorus, cutting him off, obscuring him, making him unrecognizable. Like an art restorer, I would have to expunge them from the picture in order to recover a halfway faithful portrait of my friend—whose profile had been utterly blurred by the discoveries of the past few days. His whole history as a writer, it seemed to me, had actually been a gradual self-obliteration, and the final step of physical suicide, which had seemed so desperate to us all, myself included, was for him nothing more than the ultimate fulfillment of the plan. Seeing things from this angle, I realized that the widows had a vital interest in Rudolf's "estate," which threatened to pull them into the same vortex of destruction.

Chapter 12

MY SUSPICIONS WERE MORE than justified. As soon as Marta was safely out of range, I quickly tucked away Rudolf's second novel, in the original and in the Italian translation, and exited both apartment and building without further incident. Outside, the sky had turned ash gray. Heavy clouds were pushing in from the mountains in slow-moving clumps, wet wool ready to be wrung out over the city. A light wind blew through the streets, billowing out coats, rattling awnings, and kicking plastic bags listlessly through the air: harbingers of a thunderstorm that never came. In the Corso San Maurizio, I found a café where I could work undisturbed.

Since I was already familiar with the essential features of Rudolf's novel, it was possible without much effort to find what I had hoped I wouldn't; namely, that he had inserted into his novel, more or less word for word, virtually every one of the quotes he had jotted down in the blue notebook. To avoid making the work of decoding this wholesale plagiarism unnecessarily difficult, on completing each transplant he had checked off the stolen quote in his sourcebook. Since the space after Hegel's claims about the death of art was still blank, I could be sure that none of the novel's protagonists talked like Hegel. Clearly, Hegel's literal words had not fit his work, or had been appropriated only in a paraphrase. Several hours and many cups of coffee later, I had located all of the quotations from the blue notebook in the novel and marked them, which finally brought me to the startling conclusion that fully one-third of the novel was not Rudolf's creation at all. At first I was astounded by the care and craft with which he had appropriated these disparate chunks of text, then shocked—stunned, in fact—at the insolence, the sheer nerve of this fabrication, which no one looking at the book and my notes could excuse as a montage. Might his other notebooks prove that he had excerpted the rest of the novel from other sources? I am, of course, aware that today dissertations are submitted on Jean-Paul without the author's having read all the way through one of Jean-Paul's novels. I was reminded of a friend of my youth, a man who always read ten random pages of Karl Kraus before writing his own articles, which were his but sounded like Karl Kraus's; and of course I still remember the debate that raged about a lyric poet who, without betraying his sources, had "lifted" ten images from other poets and cobbled them into a ten-line poem. He had taken the precaution of calling the result "Patchwork." So when it went on to win several prizes he was able to tell the critics who unmasked him that his title had been a deliberate clue all along. Stealing, borrowing, plundering, copying, and paraphrasing, whenever one could get away with it, were the order of the day, and perhaps it was naive for a nonwriter or a near-writer to expect that authors wishing to live from their writing could afford to wait until they thought up something that was all their own.

With Rudolf, so far as I could judge, it was a somewhat different matter. Had he not been extolled throughout the world, and by its brightest minds, specifically for the number of original ideas he managed to incorporate into a fast-paced, contemporary love story? Now it seemed that many of these ideas came word for word from Kierkegaard's *Diary of a Seducer.* Of course, he had *retouched* certain old-fashioned expressions from earlier translations so carefully that at first glance you might have taken the language for his own, but once you were on to his tricks you could see Rudolf's contribution to his own novel dwindle to almost nothing. Just how meticulous a forger he was became evident in the Italian translation, where quotations originally taken from Italian sources were translated back in such a way that the casual reader would never suspect that he was reading a line of Croce or Leopardi. In all likelihood, polyglot Rudolf had done exactly the same with the English, French, and Spanish translations he'd made of his own work. I remembered him once telling me excitedly about a university in Baden-Württemberg that planned to invite all the translators of his second novel to a symposium. "Now they'll get wise to me," he crowed happily into the telephone. "Pretty soon you'll get to see me totally naked!"

Thank heavens the project had been called off for lack of funding. Lack of funding is probably the reason most forgeries are never discovered in the first place.

All those early years I had spent with Rudolf came back to me now: Rudolf reading to me the extravagant theories of Bataille; the heretical ideas of the Romanian Cioran, who suffered from insomnia; Claude Simon's early novels, with their amazing technique of slowing down time; Horkheimer's notes on the German "twilight"—all the books that Rudolf had dragged into my apartment, with the important passages marked with slips of paper, because I had complained of the length of the books themselves. My entire education consisted of fragments, marked passages, quotes taken out of context. "You must read this!" had been Rudolf's most frequent cry in those years, or "Surely you have read this!" But, unlike Rudolf, I was never able to construct a castle, or even a half-weatherproof house, from this mountain of shards of knowledge. Today Saint-Simon, tomorrow Hamann. These bits and pieces of literature, which I read through in the evenings after work, amounted, at most, to a little hutch in which I could hide.

The clouds had cleared, and it was bright outside again, as if the lights had gone up after a performance. The faces around me were beginning to relax. How elegant the people of Turin looked. I was especially taken by the perfectly coiffed old ladies, with their spindleshanks tucked under the tables all around me, chattering away. Nietzsche (whose quotes from *Beyond Good and Evil* gave a certain distinction to Rudolf's sad heroes) had had good reason to love this town.

It was after five when I paid my bill. I would have to hide the blue notebook in my overnight bag and take out a fresh shirt, so that, externally at least, I would be equipped to listen to the talks eulogizing my late friend. With a palpable sense of relief I threw Rudolf's novel, now defaced with my notes, into one of the trash baskets with which Turin is all too well supplied.

Chapter 13

I WANTED TO GIVE MARTA a present. I knew about her life with Rudolf only through allusions to certain events or periods that left out everything else, so that my recollection of Rudolf's years in Turin were like dots that could not be connected to form a coherent image. That was why I wanted to strengthen Marta's bond with me. It had to be at my initiative: I had to surprise her with something out of the ordinary that would get her talking, a gift that would both loosen her tongue and make her think she couldn't do without me. What did she know about him? Had he let her in on his literary games, as I was already calling his forgeries? After all, for several long years she had partaken of his foul moods and extreme depressions, but also of his inexorably rising fame; she had seen his bizarre habits and those emotional freeze-ups which invariably exploded in a brawl. Had she been an innocent bystander, or a Norn, tugging him along on her fatal rope? I tended, perhaps, to overestimate her influence. But the volatile way that she kept turning up tempted me to invent a more sinister role for her. There was a Marta who was always unavailable, and a Marta who was always within reach. One Marta spoke in riddles, the other solved them. These antipodal qualities could not really be reconciled in one person. But there had to be a link between them. Maybe a tributary offering would bring that link to light.

Everything displayed in the stores was either too cheap or too expensive, too casual or too intimate. Proper gifts no longer exist, at least not in Europe. Why does a cheap-looking handbag cost the same as a flight from Hamburg to Rome? Should I get her a CD? Some perfume? The more time I spent staring at display counters, the deeper became my conviction that nothing there was worth giving. There was nothing that I would have received with pleasure. Of course, as far as I can remember I have never been given presents myself. In any case, not things one usually thinks of as presents, like cologne or a shaving brush. My own connection to gifts was dysfunctional: for years my mother gave me socks for my birthday and at Christmas, brown and gray socks. But I thought it would be unfair and silly to visit my latent anger about this on Marta. She didn't deserve socks. But what did she deserve? A question with no answer. And a possible answer wasn't going to be of much help, either, that seemed clear. So I decided the present could wait. Maybe I would buy her gloves. Gloves that would keep her fingers safe from further attempts at self-mutilation. But, given the warm weather, such a present would be difficult to explain.

When I opened the apartment door, Marta was waiting for me. She had put on a skirt (from where?), and she was wearing a pale pink blouse under a dark jacket, as if she wanted to startle me. A proxy for the widow (who was hooked up to tubes in the hospital) was waiting for the deputy of the late husband in the unfortunate couple's home. Thus all stories begin, but this story I would not be telling. ("No, no stories, anymore.") "Has something happened to Elsa?" I asked right off, imagining the worst, but instead of answering she put her index finger to her lips. She was signing me to shut up, so I did. In truth, I never wanted to say anything ever again.

Her reason for silence was sitting in the living room: an unhealthy-looking homunculus who promptly stood up and began introducing himself in a protracted, mumbled monologue. What I managed to gather from it was this: based on the suspicions of the two men from the pound, an autopsy had been performed on Caesar, with Elsa's explicit permission, and the coroner's verdict was that the dog had been poisoned. Poisoned? By whom? Us? What a fool I had been not to have shifted my activities to a neutral location. What could I possibly have had to do with Caesar's death? How could Elsa ever think I could be so villainous as to harm a poor dog whose only crime had been to think that I was Rudolf, his dear master. (That term, incidentally, for the relationship of man to animal is both revealing and revolting.)

But if it was Elsa who had denounced me to the police as a potential dog killer, why had she not accused me of more obvious villainy—that is, of wanting to enrich myself from Rudolf's literary estate? For in fact I was the only one of Rudolf's survivors who, prima facie at least, stood to profit in any way from his death. I alone had been named his executor, it was possible that I would become his editor and publisher, and no one would have the power to question any plans I might have to present his work in a too favorable or unfavorable light. By his death, Rudolf had made me an author; his suicide had elevated me to a position where I could show off my own talents. The only thing I had to worry about was keeping his female survivors from wresting fame from my grasp.

Meanwhile, the existence of the two Thai girls and the terrace had to remain our secret; however, the morose little man was insisting that I show him the dog food I had fed Caesar in Elsa's absence. But there was no dog food in the kitchen. There was only a little bag of rice and a collapsed croissant, some baking powder, sugar, and a can of coffee—*niente altro,* I said repeatedly, directly into the official's face, as it darkened with skepticism. He now proceeded to stick his nose into the baking powder. Finally, his patience exhausted, he grabbed the trash can and without further ceremony dumped its contents onto the kitchen table and started picking through the meager leftovers with a practiced hand. Some torn-up letters, cigarette butts, and a woman's frayed sandal, in which God knows why he took a particular interest. Trash. Surely even a dog murderer would not be foolish enough to dump the fatal poison in the trash.

"Old age," I said, "and grief. The dog had licked his plate clean, and then died of grief. First the master, then the dog."

And how did the dog's owner die? The supervisor wanted to know, cocking his head. I relayed the question to

Marta, since there was no way I could bring myself to give the correct answer.

"Suicide," she said. "The documents were filed with the appropriate police authorities about ten days ago."

"Was an autopsy ordered?"

"You will have to ask his wife," Marta said. "We are not family members."

"When did you last see the dog alive?" The little man now asked me, and I was glad that I could give him precise information.

"Yesterday," I said, "yesterday afternoon. By then Caesar wasn't exactly what you'd call alive any more, but he still knew me. A very old dog, almost blind, more or less deaf, coat gone, bones soft, but a dear and loyal friend who bid me a personal farewell."

"Even so, the dog got that food from somewhere," the little man insisted.

"After the owner's death and the wife's hospitalization it was your responsibility to see that the dog was fed on time—right?"

I looked over at Marta, who had assumed an impenetrable expression but still nodded and said, "*Si, credo.*" With that, the increasingly awkward interrogation was over, and the gloomy little man departed, leaving behind his visiting card.

"You'll be hearing from us."

Marta was crying. To cheer her up, I said, "I always thought you Italians could kill animals anytime you felt like it, as you do with our German songbirds." This foolish joke didn't go down too well. Caesar had been poisoned, a dismal fact that we were just going to have to live with. Who could possibly have wanted to harm Rudolf's closest friend? We solemnly swore to wait for the official report before driving ourselves crazy with speculation. Maybe the dog had eaten a poisonous plant. Perhaps the other animals had wanted to force his abdication?

After putting the garbage back into its container, we adjourned, I to shower and shave and Marta to put on her makeup: two survivors trying to mask their grief. While Marta was busy applying her black eyebrow pencil, I managed to stash the blue notebook in my overnight bag undetected.

Chapter 14

THE CEREMONY AT THE institute was well attended. Marta—although she shared her compatriots' aversion to literary readings and was amazed that in Germany, according to Rudolf, no one in the least minded sacrificing an evening to these events, even when the writers were terrible readers—was deeply moved. (Rudolf himself had been anything but a good reader: he had a tendency to revise his text while reading it, first entering into a conversation with the words and then, when they simply resisted further change, stuttering and stumbling. Nonetheless his readings were invariably always fully booked, and in some towns they had turned into cult events.) Thanks to our interrogation by the pound official, Marta and I were the last to arrive. We stood at the back of the room, where Marta was able to explain to me who was who: professors, literati, journalists, students—she recognized all of them by the backs of their heads, or by their headgear. Nearly all of the women were wearing veils or hats. There were welcome speeches, speeches full of gratitude, and even a modicum of gossip. The rhetorical skill of making a dead man vanish forever was on exhibit at the highest level. I started counting how often the words *tragic* and *tragedy* came up. And then, at last, a German colleague of Rudolf's delivered a short, intelligent talk about his work, which had made such a lasting impression in Italy as well. This was followed by well-deserved applause. Finally, to my horror, the university president asked me, as Rudolf's oldest friend and literary executor, to say a few words. I felt paralyzed. Still distracted by thoughts of Caesar, I had only vaguely taken in the president's words; now Marta had to propel me step by step to the podium. *"Say something,"* she whispered, and while those in front were turning around in their seats, wondering why Rudolf's best friend had not been seated in the front row but had apparently been hidden in back, I reeled clumsily up the middle aisle, tripping and nearly falling over a student's leg, and finally, out of breath, came to rest at the microphone. Not a pretty sight, as Marta told me later. I asked them to forgive my poor Italian (approving mumbles), regretted Rudolf's absence (suppressed laughter), and Elsa's absence (silence), talked a bit about our Berlin student commune days (I apparently expressed myself in a manner that was unintelligible, since suddenly everyone started whispering). Then I proceeded to thank Marta (this to make points with her), who, as Rudolf's closest confidante, was now helping me go over the body of the master's unpublished works, and I was more or less respectably getting out my final assessment of the irreparable loss we had suffered at the death of this great pioneer when I suddenly turned to stone. I hoped my condition would be ascribed to my grief, though the actual reason was far less banal: I had been directing my gaze to the left, so as not to seem to be addressing the empty center aisle, and there, in the front row on the far left, I discovered Eva. Eva in a hat, no doubt about it. Swathed in black, handkerchief held to her quivering lips, her solid but nice legs symmetrically rooted to the floor. Eva from Zehlendorf, now a respectable lady, blubbering away softly. Had she winked? I felt her looking at me through her streaming tears—at me, the one who hadn't made professor. Second choice, defective merchandise. But now I was the survivor, I was standing at the podium, even if words had failed me. In any case, I had nothing more to say. I raised my arms, mutely trying to excuse my inability to speak and, like a condemned man, walked slowly past the sheepish faces of my audience, down the middle aisle, and back to Marta.

"That ending was good," Marta whispered. "Most impressive," and she squeezed my arm.

I could have hit her.

Thank heaven, right after the hired quartet played its finale (Schubert, but which one?), Rudolf's German lit colleague in Turin, Luigi Forte, came up to me, with an editor from his publisher at his side. Enrico, the editor, also spoke German, and as he introduced himself I used the opportunity to slip off into a corner with the two of them and the trusty Marta.

"You must stick with me, no matter what," I begged the three of them, who looked at me worriedly. "I don't care what the seating arrangements at the dinner are, only you two or Marta may sit next to me, and no one else must speak to me, or even get near me—above all no Germans, and especially no German women. Please consider it your duty to protect me. Security Level One!" Maybe Enrico and Luigi had become accustomed to Rudolf's peculiar needs; possibly the eccentricities that had afflicted him and their other German guests and authors even amused them now and then. In any event, they both cheerfully promised to look after me. "Nothing will happen," Forte said. "You can count on us."

I could still feel the professor's reassuring hand on my arm when, from behind, someone clapped me roughly on the shoulder. Eva. She had immediately gone looking for me, shameless as she was, and now she was standing there uncertainly, dabbing her nose with a crumpled, tear-soaked handkerchief. Even in this precarious situation she did not hesitate to embrace me, and before I could hold up a hand she was hanging about my neck. I sagged a bit from the heft of her, for she, too, had gained weight over the years. It was embarrassing to be ambushed like that while we were both still technically in mourning, and even more embarrassing not to be able to explain my position. We no longer know how to keep our mouths shut, even at life's most horrific moments: we feel compelled to explain, excuse, obfuscate. The less we can do, the more we discuss our powerlessness. But by now there wasn't enough space between Eva and me to squeeze in a word.

Having witnessed this first encounter, the two Italians understood the danger I was in. Forte's expression grew grimly determined, Marta turned away in revulsion, only

Enrico tried to interfere, since he knew Eva: he had once had the dubious pleasure of translating her essay on "Women at the Easel" for an anthology his press was publishing. Now he stood at my back and spoke to her—her head was craned over my shoulder—in a kindly, imploring tone, which after some time persuaded her to loosen her grip on me. "You know," Eva said to Forte (who was totally innocent of such matters), "that I wanted to live with Rudolf?"

"But Rudolf didn't want to live with you," said Marta dryly.

Against my own will and stated intentions, I was forced to introduce the actors in this drama who were unacquainted with one another (and who, I suspected, at least in Luigi Forte's case, wanted to remain so). This unpromising exercise was interrupted by the university president, who came up to congratulate me on my outstanding talk and my excellent Italian. Eva introduced herself as a professor of art history and Rudolf's closest associate for decades, and as one whom these tragic events had prevented from carrying on important work with him.

Given his age and his position, it seemed likely the president had often met many such survivors of the famous, and he simply nodded. A tragedy, yes, he said, and offered to lead us to the dinner, which was being held at a nearby restaurant. Professor Forte would show us the way. Since Eva, without asking me, and certainly not at my instigation, took my right arm, Marta did the same with my left. So we three were as a troika, with Luigi Forte in front as our leader and Enrico behind as our beater, and thus we made our way through the evening throngs underneath the arcades to one of the best restaurants in town. At the end of the street, a half-moon hung shivering between wispy clouds, sending anxious shadows scuttling across the pavement. Had we taken a final leave of Rudolf? Or had we not yet reached the anteroom of the chamber where he lay in self-enthroned state? In any case, he would not appear at our banquet. Eva had fallen silent. And if she attempted to say something I shushed her. Not now, please. Everyone should be allotted only a limited number of spoken words per lifetime; Earth would then be a quieter place. Those who talked too much one year would have to pay a forfeit in silence the next. Twelve good months before they could turn the volume back on. Parliamentarians would have to clam up. "Quiet" restaurants, with the only sound the clatter of silverware, would be opened up everywhere.

Marta seemed to get heavier by the minute. And since I found it virtually impossible to synchronize all six of our feet into a regular rhythm, we stumbled like drunks through the evening streets of Turin. When we passed a beggar, I used the excuse to send my "partners" ahead, while I gave the man his due, then brought up the rear with Enrico. I could not believe these two totally unsynchronized women in front of us had both played important roles in my friend's intellectual life.

The truth was probably quite different. They most likely had been only prosthetic extensions of him, the feelers that Rudolf used to check whether he was still up to dealing with this world.

Chapter 15

TO BE HONEST, I HAVE NO memory of how I got back to Rudolf's apartment that night. Alone, at any rate, if everything went according to my own plans. There was a medium-sized, blood-encrusted wound on my right elbow, and my right knee was swollen, so at some point I must have had a nasty fall. My jacket, on the other hand—my only jacket—had got off lightly. It was missing only two of the three buttons from each sleeve. Buttons with no function, probably an atavistic remnant from a more military age.

I remembered that the table had emptied before midnight, which gave Eva, who had originally been seated at the end opposite mine, the opportunity to move closer. Quite unapologetically, she took full advantage of the flagging energies of the professors and their wives, and lay in wait for the departure of the president, after which she crept up on us, in her grotesque hat, which was shaped like a gigantic black snail. Clothing as a form of self-flagellation had been an inexhaustible theme with Rudolf, and the hat was its most cruel and unnatural form when worn by the wrong woman. Why Eva had to keep hers on in a restaurant—why she had to hide beneath this protective headgear—would have been the subject of a long telephone conversation with him. In the end, she had made her move and placed herself next to us. Since she had not brought her wineglasses with her, the waiter, stooping with fatigue, had to bring her fresh ones, and no sooner were they filled than she raised one and in a brief but ill-conceived speech demanded that everyone drink a toast to the deceased. Forte and Enrico then raised their glasses in a loud and clear toast to Elsa, about whom we had been talking the entire evening, and then Marta, features rigid as if numbed by Eva's tactlessness, delivered a lengthy toast to Caesar, which involved a detailed and depressing explanation of the dog's end.

It turned out that in fact none of Rudolf's colleagues who were present had known the dog. Not one had ever even set foot in the apartment. Outside of us initiates, no one had any idea of the living treasures Rudolf had collected there. Neither had they really "grasped" Rudolf, I decided. They had merely been aware of him and of his fame.

What followed remains only dimly impressed on my memory. The evening ended with my denouncing Eva vehemently in German as the vilest of legacy-hunters. Neither Professor Forte nor Enrico, and least of all Marta, saw any reason to leap to the humiliated woman's defense, and instead slipped quietly out of the restaurant, leaving me alone with Eva and our waiter, who had collapsed with exhaustion at a table nearby. I can see him now, his hands clapped over his face, ready to weep.

I think we were finally asked to leave. I can remember the rattling noises made by waiters on the Piazza San Carlo as they stacked up and chained the tables and chairs, and stray dogs, gathered beneath a giant illuminated Martini advertisement, relieving themselves against the columns of the arcade. A man approached me as I stood in the square, a man carrying a shopping bag stuffed to the seams, an ugly, monstrous thing that scraped the ground. "What a town," he shouted, as he confronted us there in the middle of the night, "what a terrific town," and proceeded to tell us the story of his life. I wanted to get away from him, but there was no gap in his verbiage where I could squeeze in my *basta.* How many times that has happened to me, being forced to listen to someone, just because I didn't think I could justify walking off. But this man had no such problem. When I finally began explaining at elaborate length that unfortunately I really had to be on my way home, he walked off without a word of regret, and I heard him exclaiming to the next passerby, "What a terrific town!" Somewhere, somehow, in all of this I must have lost Eva. But just what the circumstances were I can no longer recall.

I do remember suddenly finding myself on a park bench, and becoming aware of the aroma of fresh bread. It felt like paradise (especially without Eva!). Every day in Turin this aroma is created afresh, though its tangible results, usually soft panini, are horrible. Still, I would happily pay to inhale this warmest of all smells every day.

And then? Blackout. A gray sky, a cloth stretched between the buildings and nothingness. And once again, Eva, reappearing mysteriously, hat in hand, head bowed, looking as if she expected a beating, or had been beaten already. Was that in the Via San Pietro in the Vincoli quarter? And was the bench, which became my bed, if my memory serves me, actually in a cemetery?

Whatever had happened overnight, now that it was morning I had to consider the future—or, at least, the few days I had left in Turin, time I would have to plan carefully if I were to have any kind of extended future as the literary executor of my only friend.

Armed with a pad of notepaper and a pot of coffee, I climbed the stairs to the terrace. The sounds of the newborn day's bustle rose from the street and merged with the screech of a peacock, who lunged at me, his wings flapping in odd contortions, ill-suited to the confined space in which he lived. At this divine hour, all of creation was intent on its next meal, and from every direction strange animals came flying and running; even the tortoises, disadvantaged in every way, lumbered pitiably from their shadowy corners toward the center, toward me, who stood there facing them empty-handed. No Rudolf to stroke the dwarf rabbits' fluffy ears, no grumpy Caesar to regulate the flow of traffic—just me, benumbed and dazed, my eyes squinting in the bright light. The animals came right up to me, as if they expected something from me beyond food, a dispensation I could grant them, but I was unfamiliar with the court rituals normally practiced in this little open-air palatinate. When it became clear to them that I was not Rudolf of Assisi, and that I had nothing for them to eat, they hung their heads, making little noises of disappointment, but still stood around, confused. The chickens, one of those breeds with plumed claws, which make chickens look particularly silly, cocked their heads to one side and regarded me with wonder: how could I look so like Rudolf yet have none of his agreeable qualities? They united in protest against this pretender: they would lay no eggs today. What was I supposed to do? Getting too close to strange animals can have lethal consequences for human beings: it makes the animals bad-tempered, and then they get aggressive.

"In two hours the Thai girls will come and feed you," I said sternly. "You just have to be patient." But when I bent down to the dwarf rabbits, to run my fingers through their fur as Rudolf used to, they hopped off, insulted.

I wasn't Rudolf. But I sat down in his chair under the palm trees and wrote notes to myself on how to proceed with my work: (1.) Wangle a written power of attorney from Elsa. I wanted to handle the estate as I saw fit. It would probably be proper to have the papers signed over to me by a notary; in doing so, I would, of course, relinquish any income from the eventual sale of the rights, even though I was morally entitled to at least a portion of the expected revenues. (2.) Visit Elsa in the hospital right away. It was possible that her illness would be a prolonged one; I refused to think about a fatal outcome. The mere idea that Elsa's sister—a philistine who Rudolf said had surfaced in Elsa's life only after hearing of his fame—might resurface and interfere in the discharge of her brother-in-law's literary estate was for me a matter of great concern. (3.) Finish review of the papers promptly. I thought I might be able to use my final report on them to persuade the university to leave the complete collection in my hands, including the documents located in his offices at the university and at the institute. (4.) Weed out documents and correspondence harmful to Rudolf's reputation; bring as soon as possible back to Germany. I wanted them safe from Marta's prying. Where is nearest post office? I noted in a hasty scrawl in the margin of my agenda. Hire the Thai girls as messengers? I could not get caught going down the stairs with a lot of self-addressed envelopes. My overnight bag, though light when empty, was by now swollen with all the correspondence and notebooks that I considered to be none of posterity's business, and Marta had already cast a suspicious eye on it. Gifts, I had told her, and immediately felt around in my pants pocket for the tiny key. (5.) Expurgate Eva. I had to remove her from the story of Rudolf's life; she must not be allowed to pollute his posthumous reputation. As I scribbled her name on my little notepad, a shiver ran down my spine. Like ectoplasm in a séance, her face took shape before me, the eyebrows twitching above her cloudy gray eyes, the reddish flecks on her doughy cheeks: those same spots that had appeared, even in her youth, when she finally got up the nerve to say something but didn't quite know how to get it out, while her perpetually nervous hands wandered about her upper body or over the tabletop, looking for something to hold on to.

And suddenly, beyond the image of the woman who had taken control of my friend against his will, that other Eva appeared, the Eva who had stayed with me in Berlin after

Rudolf's departure: a gentle, somewhat dreamy creature, with round, questioning eyes, who couldn't understand why the whole world was suddenly interested in the revolution, or why she herself, instead of gazing at Raphael's Madonnas, should get worked up about the social history of the Renaissance. She had not been designed for the pettifoggery of debating groups or for the firebrand missions of politics, and she had had no sympathy at all for people who lacked a naive openness toward, or firm conception of, beauty. While we affected an air of genius and originality, employing dubious rhetoric to seem cleverer and more in charge than we really were, she had sat among us engrossed in her own thoughts, her face in a meditative pout: neither an angel nor a saint, but someone who derived a quiet strength from the contemplation of angels and saints.

I thought of her total lack of coquettishness back then, the absence of all the pretension that Rudolf had so much of—Rudolf, the literary omnivore who indeed had read everything ever written, right up to and including what he called the harebrained inventions of our contemporary novelists. Of course, there were exceptions among them: his whole life was filled with exceptions. Thus, with typical stuttering brilliance he had once declared a peculiar book by Helmut Heissenbüttel, *D'Alembert's End,* to be *the* modern novel of our time, and had delivered a long, excruciating lecture on the principle of literary collage. Trusting souls that we were, under his direction we studied the arid lessons of the materialist philosophers, along with the less dry ones, thank goodness, of Diderot, in order to acquire at least a narrow grounding for the comprehension of *D'Alembert's End,* which he finally allowed us to read for ourselves. That was the crowning moment of Rudolf's imperious pedagogy. There was no mention, or practically no mention, made of D'Alembert in Rudolf's sourcebook—only the quotation that Thomas Mann took as epigraph for *Doktor Faustus:* "Quotations of this kind have something musical about them, disregarding the innate mechanical quality. They are, moreover, reality transformed into fiction, fiction that absorbs the real, and thus a strangely protean and attractive mingling of the spheres."

Eva had not been at all enthusiastic about Heissenbüttel's novel, and as she brought forth her arguments I had allied myself, entrenched myself, with Rudolf. She had barely finished speaking, however, when Rudolf the ringmaster, employing that special nastiness of which he was capable, ripped her opening statement to shreds. "*D'Alembert's End* is recycled literature," he yelled at her, "and yet you want it to be complete and whole unto itself!" Nobody knew what he meant by that: the novel as recycled literature. Back then, in 1970, anything was possible. Later, when Rudolf had abandoned Heissenbüttel and started on a new course, "Mathematical Economics: *Kapital* Volume III," she finished her earlier argument, a respectful but harsh critique of *D'Alembert's End,* with which I agreed in every respect. "A book that simply refuses to be read, fights it tooth and nail": that phrase has stayed in my ear. Many years later, Rudolf, with me as his escort, paid a call on Heissenbüttel himself. The author had had a stroke and was sitting in a wheelchair that seemed much too small. A great, broken man with a shaved head, he listened to Rudolf's fulsome praises in silence. I can still see his one hand twitching occasionally (his other arm had been amputated during the war), as if it were trying to express the words he could not speak but was powerless to represent anything beyond a scrawled comma. Both writers shared an uncomfortable love of Rudolf Borchardt, whom Rudolf always described to me as the only gentleman in German literature, while ordering me never to reveal this admiration to anyone. What had become of Helmut Heissenbüttel, that productive and inspired novelist and essayist, of whose work Rudolf had possessed more than thirty volumes? Now they'd been left to me: essays, poems, and collages—an entire shelf full of books with strange titles, among them the one I had always found particularly illuminating: *If Adolf Hitler Had Not Won the War.* And what would become of Rudolf, once the world's shock at his death had dissipated? Would his name and his books also fall into the sea of footnotes, flotsam and jetsam no longer permitted in the court of Now? The power to protect him from such a fate lay with me, at least for as long as I was alive. Rudolf—I could feel it clearly—was in my hands.

I had to speak to Eva. I needed to find out why, after all the humiliation she had suffered from Rudolf, after all his wrongheaded, supercilious criticism of everything she liked, she had wanted to be near him again, why she had sought him out. Why had she been willing to give up her own marriage, which, while not exactly free and easy, was at least stable, and to break up another equally complicated, also stable marriage? Why, when she was only a few years away from a well-paid retirement as professor emerita, had she even contemplated giving up her chair prematurely to live with an old man lost in his papers, a man whom the careful, sensitive reading of a lifetime would not prevent from calmly walking up to and embracing his own death? It must have been Rudolf's doing, his persuasion, just as, years before, he had persuaded me to use certain secret sources to get him the poison. The letters from him, filled with extortive references to our lifelong friendship, begging me to procure a very specific vegetable poison "for any eventuality," were in a safe place in my apartment. But I could not remember whether I had enclosed a letter, along with the plainly wrapped little package, that in my ignorance of his real motives I had sent to Turin. If there was such a note, it was unlikely that Rudolf had destroyed it, so I absolutely had to find it. Especially if Elsa decided to turn the unpublished works over to me, that letter must never see the light of day. If it did exist, I thought, Rudolf had been quite capable of deliberately hiding it in any book that came to hand, leaving its eventual discovery to chance. He had always loved such nasty games. I had to talk to Eva, but first must see Elsa. I couldn't afford to leave anything to chance.

Chapter 16

I HAVE NEVER QUITE BEEN able to imagine what might induce a person to become a professional writer. I can understand someone writing the occasional poem. Given the right state of emotional confusion, the idea might well appeal—to illuminate a segment of that dark planet of the as yet unsaid with one's very own words. Even if the poem is never published—which, aside from a few famous exceptions, is what happens—it is still in the world through the poet's effort. Even writing an essay on a noble subject, some highbrow development of one's secondary school themes, is a worthy proposition. But when someone early in life, after dropping out of, or, in rare cases, actually completing, a university course in literature or business then makes the decision to spend his or her adult life making up cops-and-robbers tales, or stories that are cannibalizations of the author's own life, that, it seems to me, is an act of sheer recklessness. Painters and musicians have it easier, in the sense that they can study at institutions set up especially for their disciplines, and complete the works that some master left unfinished. No one thinks it odd if a young composer seeks to snatch his first laurels with a variation on a theme of Zemlinsky or Bach, but if a writer should offer a variation on the ending of *The Man Without Qualities* as his debut, he would be laughed out of town. Again, a painter can become a darling of modern-art specialists by spreading broad smears of paint over some great image of Western art, leaving only the edges peeking out; no poet could hope to achieve long-term success by simply replacing the nouns he didn't care for in Rilke's *Sonnets to Orpheus.* Novelists in particular ply an extremely risky trade. What happens when someone has successfully crossed the one-track bridge to artistic maturity and wants to publish novels that are out of step with the current taste of critics or the public? Here I do not refer to how others will value the artistic truth of the work, which as a rule is recognized only once the artist is dead. No, I mean the value assigned—or not—to the sheer effort. There he sits (like Rudolf), year in and year out, obsessed with detail, slaving away at an ever growing mound of paper, and in the end he is forced to admit that even in his own estimation all he has produced is nonsense. To be sure, in the meantime there are public or semi-public support programs encouraging a disillusioned novelist with financial enticements to try again a second or even a third time. But beyond that? As I accompanied Rudolf on his reading tours, I came across lots of writers who at fifty were essentially unemployed, either because their publishers had given them notice following a decline in critical and public interest in their work or because they had simply run out of material. These has-beens would relate the story of their failed careers with the most passionate literary conviction, and sometimes I got the feeling that their tales of ultimate failure were truer to life than all the so-called success stories that other, wilier prose writers could manufacture at will. Here was rich material for those who had written themselves out on happier themes: marriages wrecked, philosophies discredited, hopes of financial and professional success gone south. Not a few of them attempted to turn their lives around again with a painstaking depiction of their disappointments and shortcomings. But since most of these authors lacked any sense of self-irony their tales of misfortune were no more compelling than a social worker's case studies—or hopeless-case studies—and unremarkable even within that genre. Sad creatures.

One of them has remained in my memory. He was a melancholy gentleman with elegant manners, impeccably dressed despite his reversals, who accompanied us to an Italian restaurant after a reading Rudolf gave at an adult-education center near Cologne. Ducking his head as he spoke, as if he were permanently abashed, he described in exquisite language his vain efforts to add a second chapter to his third novel, the first chapter of which he had completed years before but was still constantly revising. Twenty pages were finished, but the remainder, which he estimated at about four hundred pages, simply would not start. "It refuses to come to me," he exclaimed, laughing hysterically, "and I clearly have no bait to lure it. Did bait mean experience, I asked him, interrupting his desperate mirth, but this question brought such a pitying smile to his face that I did not contribute another word to the conversation. "Sometimes I spend entire days," he replied, "thinking about whether the main character should make his own dinner or whether I should send him into a restaurant. If he goes to a restaurant, there's always the danger that the novel will be thrown off track, because the hero might fall in love or get drunk and wake up in jail. Since, to my great regret, I have never done time, I would have to imagine the experience, which would spoil the story's authenticity, or I would have to leave his jail cell undescribed. If he gets his own meal at home, on the other hand, his fussiness gets on my nerves. He spends hours washing dishes because he has nothing else to do. Everything he does is just an outgrowth of his existential nothingness, which is, in turn, hard to express on paper. You would not believe how much I have written about trash disposal and then thrown out! I've had to destroy a long chapter where he washes his clothes in a sink, even though that was meant to be my definitive treatment of the theme of self-purification. It was a disaster. It was awful!"

Rudolf—I still remember—recommended an extensive reading program of Montaigne and Homer, allegedly an incendiary combination of subjective and objective elements that would get him quickly back to his desk, then paid the bill, which, given the writer's enormous consumption of wine, was not inconsiderable, and finally presented the poor devil with the remainder of his honorarium for the reading. A few years later, Rudolf, who had continued to take a touching interest in the man, told me that the poor though impeccably dressed author had finally got hired as professor of creative writing at a college in Iserlohn, which officially relieved him of the necessity of writing the second chapter of his third novel. His lecture plan was ready-made: built upon himself as the prime example *ex negativo.* Incidentally, just a few weeks before his own death, Rudolf wrote to me that he was going to push for the reissue of this writer's first two novels, which he considered to be towering examples of great narrative art of the seventies, an unbeatable combination of Beckett and Robert Walser. Beckett's hoboes and Walser's boulevardiers did meet, after all, in that pub known as the Absent God. Meanwhile, constrained by my job and its duties up to my early retirement, I'd never got around to reading those two novels, but now I looked forward to seeing the new editions, with afterwords by Rudolf containing, so he told me, a reminiscence of our shared meeting—including my naive question about experience. At one point, Rudolf had explained to me that having one's eyes opened even once should provide enough material for a multivolume Collected Works.

But if it was not an inner need to relate experiences, including negative, painful, perhaps even traumatic experiences, that drove a young person to give up all middle-class safety nets and take up writing as a profession, then what was it? I found it impossible to imagine a reasonably happy, semi-complacent human being, comfortably embedded within a traditional family, hitting on the daring idea of writing, even as a pastime, a novel such as *America, The Man Without Qualities,* or *Joseph and His Brothers.* Was it for the sheer joy of creation? Or for sporting reasons, to inspire one's depressed, blocked colleagues, show them how easy it is to continue composing the great Psalm of Beauty?

Rudolf always insisted that his own writing was basically nothing but an attempt to free himself from the illusion that he was a writer. "You have to keep at it long enough to be one hundred percent sure that you are not," he would say. "Alas, most give up before that. But a real writer can only come out of the ashes of a destroyed writing career." All the others, he believed, were merely producing texts, mostly texts on commission. Only the daily cruel experience of defeat in this game of words and sentences mattered, not the easily won victories. On numerous occasions he told me, more or less in confidence, that his novels, published all over the world, awarded prizes, and sold for a fortune to international movie companies, were not exactly total crap, perhaps, but still so unimportant, so insignificant and tasteless in the profoundest sense that all the fuss made about his work was deeply embarrassing to him. He actually held the view that his books were among the elect only because everything else was worse. The high and low points of any novel are attained by chance, but when all the rest is nothing but undisciplined hackwork, then we are at the end of literature as art. "In my work," he often said, "you can feel the influence of world literature, and that's why so many readers trust it." Back then, of course, I didn't know that these books, so well written and beautiful to read, originated in borrowings from other writers, writers who had struggled their entire lives, sometimes in vain, to obtain the recognition that Rudolf had been granted in excess. I had believed his novels were original work, as had millions of other readers. I could remember conversations I had had with Rudolf on the sickness of writing. You can't just stop, was his theory. In fact, even if you do stop writing and publishing you will still be a writer. Between the written or the yet-to-be-written text and its author, there is a morbid complicity over which outside opinion has no power. On the contrary, writers who have stopped writing are usually artistically superior to those who keep on writing in order to hide their illness from the public. The public has no idea that writing is a disease, and that the writer who publishes is like the beggar who exhibits his sores. The illness of those who no longer publish (either because they have nothing to say or because they simply don't want to say it anymore) at least is not shamelessly on display. Either way, we are left with writing as an incurable sickness that can be ended only by death.

Chapter 17

AND NOW TO ELSA.

I'd had some difficulty getting away from the terrace, since a mallard drake with a shimmering green collar around his neck, evidently a bachelor cruising for a duck, had flown in and after several unsuccessful attempts at landing elsewhere had finally plopped himself onto my table and made himself at home. Disappointed in his mating, he settled for a little nap in the morning sun: first he spread out his wings in a sort of avian stretching exercise, then he nestled his head within the resulting cavity. One eye still looked out at me intently; I was unsure whether this gaze was of friend or foe. Did the eye see Rudolf, or me? Now and then a flap of tissue slid across the black, shiny pupil, but that didn't mean its owner had ceased to observe me. I hardly dared breathe, let alone write.

Just like a public beach, I thought, where human beings spread their towels out and without so much as a hello to their neighbors cavalierly remove their clothes and drop them in the sand, then stretch out naked and fall asleep as if they were all alone in the world. And woe betide you if you disturb them in any way!

Just so, whenever I started to move my pencil the drake would blink at me, as if offended. I imagined that, given his limited field of vision, he found the motions of writing displeasing. Maybe he sensed that I was stronger than he; nevertheless he wanted me to know that this hectic scribbling was not in keeping with the dignity of a drake at rest.

Promptly at ten, the Thai housemaids came up to the terrace and one of them put an end to this standoff, seizing the bird by his pretty abdomen with both hands and tossing him quickly into the air. The creature squawked loudly during this rough treatment and shook his head violently, as drakes will, but then docilely took his place in the lineup of breakfast-seekers that came scuttling out from their shadowy refuges, surrounding the two girls and appealing for food.

The two Thai girls would not be much use for my errands, I decided. The word *post,* common to almost all European languages, was unknown to them, and the more I repeated it, explaining it with gestures, the louder their high-pitched laughter got, which in turn caused the animals to perform the most bizarre imitations of them. All the world's a stage, it seems. Through the power of mimesis, the little zoo suddenly became a circus, though all I had said was "post." I wondered what the girls would have made of the notebooks and letters from Rudolf's personal effects that I was smuggling out of the country. But they did know the names of all the various animal feeds, which they helpfully recited from memory. Perhaps they thought *post* was one of those.

When I left the building, there were several police cars standing out front; I had heard the sirens from the terrace. A flawlessly uniformed carabiniere at the front door studied me ostentatiously, but then simply let me go through. He had hooked both thumbs in his white patent-leather belt, and merely wagged his index finger to keep me from asking questions. *Move on and keep your mouth shut.* As rattled as if I were the criminal they sought, I nearly tripped on the three steps that connected the institute with the street, twisting my ankle painfully as I landed. Looking back, I saw the cop grin. Why? I thought, then censored all further thought on the subject.

I took the bus. Even at this hour of the morning, the city had already gone to work, living up to its reputation. Everything was in motion; in the coffee bars, people were taking last gulps of their coffee, grabbing their croissants to finish on the run. Traffic was jammed. It pleased me that the bus moved no faster than the pedestrian traffic; you could keep people company for a while on their way to the office. If you caught the eye of a passerby, one of two things generally happened: either he looked away, as though embarrassed at being caught walking at a pace too fast, too undignified, or he gave you the losing racer's parting scowl as you pulled past.

The weather began to change: a gray veil fell over the cinnamon-colored clouds, the light grew first colder, then hazier, and as we left the center of town the first few raindrops were starting to smudge the side windows of the bus. Up to now, I had seen nothing of the rest of the city. Not the new museum, where Eva was now doing her research, pulling together material for her final years of teaching; no churches; not even the old Fiat factory in Lingotto, though it had been the setting of one of Rudolf's novels. Even the book *Nietzsche in Turin,* which I had acquired because it contained a map with all the places the suicide-philosopher had visited or mentioned, was still in my overnight bag, unopened, pushed farther down by the documents I kept adding. I probably wouldn't read it till I got home, at which point it would be a souvenir of my unhappy time in this town.

I exited the bus and began walking through the streets with my head down, studying the pavement. Suddenly I knew for certain that once I left this city I would never visit it again. After my duties as literary executor were done, I would be through with Turin.

It was the right weather for a hospital visit. In the few meters from the bus stop to the hospital, I got soaked to the skin by a squall—it doused me as if giving me a final warning. The faces of the cigarette-smoking amputees at the covered entrance were expressionless as they watched me arrive. One man in a wheelchair, swathed in bandages, with a tiny aperture for a cigarette left in his head cast, was seated so awkwardly by the doorway that he was continually jostled by those coming in as well as those going out. Nobody thought to move him.

At a kiosk on the ground floor I bought a long-stemmed rose and a box of biscotti. The saleswoman looked like a permanent fixture in the ward. She had worn-looking Band-Aids on both hands and a high rubber collar around her neck. "Car accident, no seat belt" was her hoarsely whispered response to my concerned inquiry. I assumed her husband had beaten her up; I told her to keep the change. In town I had once seen a small Gypsy beggar hunched on the ground with her tiny naked child: she, too, had had on a rubber collar, one that was much too big for her. "That head is simply stuck on top of the collar," I said to myself. "Her real head is hidden inside the rubber wrapping." The child, to all appearances, was dead. Later Marta would insist that these pietà performers belonged to the Mafia and were schooled in special training centers to play on our sympathy. "Everything in Italy that evokes your pity is staged by the Mafia," she said. "The Gypsies learn that sidelong glance and how to have the shakes. And the babies are taught how to look dead. If they smile or laugh, they get batted on the head. Not until evening, back in their cozy villas counting their money, can they act naturally." In any case, as we were sitting safely on a bus at the time, I could do nothing about the awful scene except avert my eyes.

The elevator to the fourth floor was tightly packed, and passengers continued to board at every stop. My nose was pressed against the nearly bald skull of a woman in a bathrobe, who got out with me. She was crying. I wanted to give her a hug.

Through the glass door, second room on the right. A nurse murmured something unintelligible as she took away my rose, so now all I had in my hand was a box of cheap biscotti. I dropped it on an empty hospital bed in the hallway. I couldn't bear the thought of pretending to cheer Elsa up with a roll of cookies. A rose and some cookies, maybe, or even a rose alone, but cookies and nothing else—that was embarrassing. "*Cinque minuti,*" said the nurse, holding up five fingers, obviously recognizing that I was a foreigner.

So I had exactly five minutes to try to put my future life in order. If I got Elsa's signature, I could take everything with me to Germany and hand down my own picture of Rudolf to posterity. If I didn't, I would have to handle matters another way.

Elsa was asleep. Her roommate had been taken elsewhere, or perhaps death had come for her. The presence of death in the room was palpable, its touch was everywhere: in the lacquer-painted walls, in the open wardrobe and the empty bed, loosely covered with a wrinkled spread, in the crucifix next to the window. And death had told Elsa his plans for her, too. As I seated myself on her sad little bed, she briefly opened her eyes. A twitch of her mouth showed that she had recognized me, but her bony hand made no sign. She was already on her way.

I looked down at her for a long while. From the expression on her face, you could see that she was no longer sure whether she still belonged to this world or was already in the other. All the trouble that had been visible in her eyes (now quivering beneath their lids) was gone. You couldn't even hear her breathe. One thing about Elsa had always struck me: her looks changed instantaneously, from moment to moment. In a kind of automatic reflex her carefree, smiling girl's face would become a somber mask, impassive as her silence at such times, then—snap!—she'd change again, to the serious, cultured, engaged *professoressa* expounding on the incomprehensibilities of the world. Among her many other faces, there was one I particularly liked: her face when she sang Italian lullabies. Elsa had taken great pains to create the first anthology of Italian children's songs, and had published it in two volumes, with commentary. Rudolf always got a sardonic expression on his face when she sang these ditties, to her guitar or at the piano, and you couldn't quite tell whether it was because he couldn't sing himself, because they didn't have any children, or simply because he couldn't stand to see everyone's attention concentrated on Elsa. While she was singing, he and his genius ceased to exist. Sometimes he would even voice the suspicion that their few friends visited them only because of her, came only to hear her sing—which was certainly not the whole truth but might not have been that far off.

Should I wake Elsa now and ask her for her signature? I had the document all ready; she would only have to sign it. She did not even need to be fully conscious; I could move her hand for her.

In fact, though, Elsa had always had a phobia about thieves. This traumatic fear—which had led to incredibly complicated dead bolt–locking procedures in the apartment—originated on the one hand with a childhood experience that I never really quite understood, and on the other with the loss of her *Habilitationsschrift,* her postdoctoral thesis, written in German. This manuscript, taken to the post office personally by Rudolf and sent as registered mail, never arrived at the university in Frankfurt, and the carbon copy

Elsa had kept in her Turin office had vanished as well. This double disappearance was discussed from every angle in the media; every speculation on this attempt to derail an academic career was explored, including the vilest one: that Rudolf was behind it. Elsa, who had previously published all the chapters of her extensive study in academic periodicals, received her appointed lectureship in Frankfurt based retroactively on those writings, but her dread of thieves remained. So it was, alas, completely out of the question for me to ask her, in her current condition, for that all-important signature.

When my five minutes were up, I left the pallid room. Three times, at long intervals, I had whispered her name. At least she could keep her name. On my way out, I noticed the roll of biscotti still resting on the bed in the hallway. I left it there.

Chapter 18

WHEN I RETURNED TO Rudolf's apartment, Marta, all-knowing, all-seeing, was there to receive me. Her triumphant air and look of contempt did not bode well, nor did the fact that as I walked in she did not bother to stand up to greet me; this lack of basic courtesy made me a little panicky. I could not help thinking that I stood before her as the accused, and that she, seated, was the state's attorney. To banish this image, I walked casually over to the kitchen to make some coffee. My stroll across the room felt like a move in a chess game, and I desperately pondered whether this opening gambit would lead to victory; I couldn't think of one to follow it that didn't threaten immediate checkmate—mine, that is. Marta's role in the world was to drive me out of it. I remembered a game I had often played with Rudolf: deciding which individuals must be eliminated from one's life to clear the deck for one's own free development. In my case, only Marta had to go.

The tiny espresso machine had just started sputtering when I sensed her behind me. She was leaning against the door frame, ankles crossed, arms folded. I would probably have to come to some kind of agreement with her, just as she—clever woman—had unceremoniously allied herself with me. But I wanted to resist. I wanted to solve the problem of Rudolf without her.

"The police have cleared out Rudolf's office," she said. "A temporary measure." At first I didn't understand what she meant. "There is a risk that documents belonging to the institute might disappear," she explained. "If you want any of the papers here in the apartment, you'd better hurry."

I turned on the light, to see her more clearly, then turned it right off. Her face resembled a quince—muddy yellow, hard, and misshapen. I felt the cup in my hand start to shake, but I walked bravely on past her to my room. My bag looked untouched, stuffed, and ready to travel.

I was back at the table again, working on a new box of letters, when I heard the apartment door slam. I was sorting through some fan mail: an edition of Rudolf's letters would certainly be a sensation. I couldn't judge from the occasional obscene notes Rudolf had jotted on these letters, which themselves left little to the imagination, whether he had written back. Why hadn't he simply consigned such unfortunate screeds to the wastebasket? I was amazed at the offhand manner in which women, most of them his countrywomen but all of them complete strangers, would offer themselves to Rudolf: *You have described my problem as if you knew me. Wouldn't you like to get to know me in reality?* That was the message. Since nature has devised only ten variations on Central Europeans, our own fate seems to crop up in at least every tenth German novel. Many of these ladies offered to combine their next vacation trip with a pilgrimage to his university; others gave a Positano hotel address, wondering if a call from him would save them from the longueurs of their holiday; still others had simply written their mobile phone numbers on a blank sheet of paper. One woman had even given him her scheduled arrival time in Turin and the name of the hotel she planned to spend the night in, and from Rudolf's marginal notes it seemed probable that he had actually met her, or at least that he hadn't been disinclined to do so: "Seminar?" "Elsa in Rome." On another letter, sent by "Dörte" from Celle, who in her vulgar candor was more than willing to give him "all," he had written "Reading in Hamburg May 17." The sheer bulk of these letters horrified me. I felt uneasy and abandoned, but most of all disillusioned that Rudolf had received this kind of mail. Clearly I was not cut out to be a voyeur, and I now realized that I could not even begin to fulfill my job as a literary executor without a healthy dose of exactly that kind of curiosity. The technical challenges scared me, too: Would I now be required to inform all of these women that their epistolary outpourings would soon be made available for public viewing in the archive at Marbach? Didn't I also have to ask them whether they would make Rudolf's answers available to me for the eventual publication of his collected letters? The mere idea of having to correspond with so many neurotic females suggested an alternative strategy: to destroy the contents of these boxes without reading further.

Wouldn't Rudolf have done the same? The volume of the epistolary part of his estate would probably shrink by about twenty percent, and this would naturally reduce its value, but I had already culled enough correspondence of a less lurid nature to prove how influential Rudolf's books had been on his readers.

For the time being, I returned the carton to its proper place in the architecture of gray boxes, taking the next one right away, to distract myself from thoughts of the other confiscation program I was planning, which, after all, would affect a much larger portion of my friend's literary estate.

What was it about Rudolf that had charmed so many people? Where was the magnetism in a sixty-year-old German professor in Turin who burrowed around in weighty tomes and raved about Pascal? Even granting that a widely published writer whose novels seem custom-made for certain readers has a greater attraction than the average person who tells ordinary stories in mundane private conversations, that didn't explain the enormous stream of mail from women who felt that Rudolf had "understood" them. Had there been among them admirers who, like Eva, still felt the wish to "give him all" even after meeting him? Or had the famous author of a few novels of ill-fated love been reduced by a cup of coffee in the Turin train station, or even a night in an obscure hotel, to an ordinary man who after a few dubious attempts to amuse his conquest took off and was forgotten? After all, even Rudolf's life, no less than the lives of the women who pursued him, consisted largely of emptiness, of boring repetition. Yet clearly he had managed to present his life's banalities as a great mystery. And, just as clearly, he had frittered away his time leading these multiple lives, giving each of his few trusted friends the impression that he or she was part of his real, true life, never letting them suspect the existence of all the others. As for me, the more I found out about him the less I felt I knew him. Once I had read his correspondence, I realized that Rudolf had been playing us all for fools. Put another way, he had betrayed all of us, and then, just in time, slipped away.

Or was I simply envious, having lived only one life myself? After my apprenticeship as a printer and further training as a *Kulturwirt* in international economics and culture, I had been preoccupied with earning a living, and it was only because the state-subsidized institute that employed me had been closed—for financial reasons—that I had been able to retire early and could now think about beginning another life. But it looks slightly ridiculous when an older man tries to do this. Maybe I didn't have enough imagination. Or enough money. Or, maybe, enough nerve. Rudolf had always urged me to "take pen in hand" and write a great novel on the cultural bureaucracy—"the culture industry," as he put it—since in his opinion I was up to snuff in such matters. "Of course, you'll make yourself a lot of enemies," he'd said, "but it's better to start with a few good enemies for life when you are beginning your real career so late." Unfortunately, my attempts to write from experience never amounted to more than a few dry essays. I've had my own love affairs, and some of them have enriched my life, some impoverished it.

And Eva, who had literally fallen into my lap?

I can still see her, sitting across from me at the old kitchen table in Berlin, her chin resting on her fists, a strand of hair falling over her right eye, a copy of Siegfried Gideon's *Mechanization Takes Command* before her. "You must not try to be like Rudolf," she said, taking my protesting hand, "because you will never be like Rudolf. You can't share his lust for life, because it's foreign to you."

Of course, I denied ever even thinking about imitating Rudolf, but I could feel my ears turning red. "Promise me," Eva had said solemnly, and since she seemed determined not to let go of my hand until I did, I limply, awkwardly, said, "I promise."

Chapter 19

BEFORE I GOT TOO INVOLVED with the last of the boxes Rudolf had designated as his literary testament, I needed to get up and stretch my legs. I carefully bolted the door, opened my overnight bag, and, in a panic at the thought of being caught, took all the documents to and from Rudolf that I had already selected, stuffed them into envelopes, and packed the envelopes inside two plastic shopping bags. Then I crept to the stairway and stood there for a long while, listening for footsteps, and heard nothing except an occasional burst of the students' laughter in the echoing hallway. As yet they knew nothing about me, their late professor's only friend. When I reached the floor where Marta's office was, I could hear her on the phone, using a voice that filled me with trepidation. She had clearly succumbed to a fit of bad temper. Suddenly I resolved to leave the city the next day. I would not and could not subject myself to Marta's bullying anymore.

Out on the street, I walked through the crowd with my head down, imagining that I was passing the people I had seen that morning from the window of the bus. I hoped none of them would recognize me. The handles of those loaded plastic sacks were cutting into my fingers: the theft that would save Rudolf's reputation weighed heavily in my hands. Marta's icy tones, Elsa's moribund whisper, and Eva's soft pleading merged in a chorus that drove me onward, when, more than once, I was tempted to drop the bags into one of the trash baskets that punctuated the street, then hang out in a bar waiting for one of the city works trucks to come and empty it. But Turin looked so neat: it would take all night for the street cleaners to come.

The post office in the train station was open. I bought some stick-on labels, wrote my own address on them, and then, my heart pounding, I sent the dozen padded envelopes off by registered post. In two days they would be in my mailbox at home.

And afterward? Suddenly I was certain that I would never do anything about them; I wanted nothing more to do with Rudolf, ever. But there he was, inside of me, a part of me, and if no one ripped him out of me I would have to drag him around with me until I died. Now that Rudolf was dead, I was Rudolf. I would either have to take the rap for all his awful stories and escapades or bring them to an end whether I wanted to or not. Everything I was rebelled against this idea, and I stopped in my tracks in the middle of the station, distraught, trying to catch my breath. People barged into me with heavy luggage, a child who clearly had lost his parents clung to my leg, a pitch-black dog stopped right in front of me, gazing at me anxiously. "Caesar," I shouted at him, and with that I broke the spell that had gripped me.

I joined the long line at the ticket counter. Amazing, how many people wanted to leave Turin with me, and like me they were all ordinary-looking citizens. One stout woman had a cage of songbirds with her, and they alone were loudly protesting their imminent change of domicile.

While I was spelling out the name of my destination to the ticket agent, a man whose knowledge of German did not extend to umlauts, someone tapped me on the shoulder. This touch had a familiar feel to it, and somehow I had expected it. I did not look up right away, but paid for my ticket and stuffed the change into my wallet.

"Are we traveling back together?" asked Eva, when I finally turned and looked her in the eye. She was wearing the same outfit she'd had on the previous day; it now looked totally wrong, but at least she'd omitted that ridiculous hat.

"Not today," I answered. "But someday soon, perhaps."

We gave each other a long, friendly hug, wasting no more words. And we parted, heading in separate directions. I did not turn around again.

Even so, I knew that her eyes followed me all the way to the exit.

Chapter 20

THERE WAS A NOTE STUCK in the apartment door. Marta wanted me to call her at home—urgent. Everything was always urgent when it came to Marta. Maybe she had an urgent need to torment me. A man answered the telephone, gruffly, but my Italian was not up to understanding what he said. "Marta," I shouted into the receiver several times. "I want to talk to Marta, do you understand?" I heard him lay down the receiver and say, with a growl, *"Qualque straniero."* Some foreigner. At last Marta came to the phone. Elsa was dead. She told me this in the same subdued voice she'd used two days earlier to tell me about Caesar. Even this block of ice melts when faced with death, I thought. Elsa had died yesterday, Marta said. Heart failure following a pulmonary embolism. She wanted to come over right away to discuss the "new situation" with me; besides, she was afraid. "We are the last two witnesses, you know?" *One too many,* it occurred to me then, but I didn't say so out loud, although I suddenly felt like putting her to the test. Something of her own temperamental nature must have rubbed off on me, just as Rudolf's moodiness and mendacity had rubbed off on her. The only trait denied a major role in our drama was candor.

"What will your husband say if you spend the night away from home again?" I asked.

"I have no husband, if that's what you'd like to hear."

Nothing. That was what I wanted to hear. And I didn't want to say anything, either.

All I wanted was to be alone. There was one more carton in that mountain of lies that I had to go through, and then I would write my final report and be gone. Now that I knew Elsa would never learn of those carefully recorded, meticulously filed indiscretions that Rudolf had included in his literary testament—though she had probably suspected them all along—the only thing that mattered to me was keeping this deceit-saturated pile of papers from the public eye—even against Rudolf's own wishes. There was no way I was going to argue over their significance with the president of the University of Turin or the director of the archive at Marbach. They had meaning only for me—for Elsa, Eva, Marta, and me. I was the only person who had the right to forbid Rudolf to indulge his last shamelessly narcissistic impulse, his desire to burden his fellow men with his failings, even from beyond the grave. I went through all the earlier boxes one more time and removed as much material as I could fit into my bag, concentrating on any suggestive exchanges or notes Rudolf had made for letters that he meant to write later.

The answer to the overarching question of why in heaven's name he'd wished to initiate total strangers into the secrets of his strange life lay in the last box. I took the last bottle of Barolo from the pantry and opened the windows, for during the continuous rain the room had grown stuffy. A loud wave of traffic noise burst into the study, as if until then the city itself had been in a state of suspense, waiting for the rain to end. Although it was past eleven, even the phone began to ring; it rang incessantly. Several voices were preserved for posterity on the answering machine; other callers hung up when commanded by Rudolf's voice to leave a message. So Rudolf was still present. I closed the windows, shot the security bolt on the main door, moved the telephone to Elsa's room, and swaddled the burbling answering machine in a thick wool blanket. Then I put on a CD of Beethoven sonatas and turned the volume up so high that no other noise could disturb my nocturnal labors. The police would have to break into the apartment to put a stop to my machinations.

The last box contained six blue cardboard portfolios, each secured by a thick rubber band. I arranged them before me like tokens in some esoteric game and looked down on them uncertainly, my eyes wide open, afraid I might open the wrong one first. Could it be that Rudolf had set up the boxes so that I would be sure to find this particular box last? But hadn't Marta said that she had arranged the material for me?

The portfolios had been labeled in Rudolf's handwriting. Five bore names: Elsa's, Eva's, Marta's, Rudolf's, and mine. The sixth one was marked: *The Testament. The Torino*

Comedy. A Novel. The word *The* before *Torino Comedy* had been crossed out, then stetted. About the main title, too, Rudolf seemed to have been undecided. He had struck through the definite article several times, replacing it with *A;* The variants *A Torino Testament* and *Torino Testament* had also been considered, but ultimately the original formulation, with the two definite articles, had won out; it struck me as the least elegant. Rudolf had circled the words *The Testament. The Torino Comedy. A Novel* with a broad red marker. So this was his last novel, the one he'd been sure would set the entire genre on its head: this thin little folder containing perhaps fifty pages, on which he had allegedly worked for years, if not decades—a nothing, a paltry joke, a disaster, a declaration of aesthetic bankruptcy.

I felt literally sick; my stomach was turning. How could he have deceived himself and us so completely for so long, and then taken his own life? All those years of study, all the nerve-racking preparation, the dizzying intellectual constructions, and then . . . this thin blue folder with its handful of pages, not much more than a long letter of the sort he had written so often in his youth. A shrunken universe. I saw how the lie had spread over his face and slowly corroded it.

And then I opened the folder. The title again, without corrections, but supplied with a date: Completed 2004. On the next page was the table of contents, divided into twenty chapters: Shame, War, Honor, Betrayal, Breakthrough, and so on, up to Farewell. It fit exactly on one page and had no corrections of any kind, a beautiful image made calligraphically appealing by Rudolf's flowing hand. On the next page, two mottoes: the first a quote from Maurice Blanchot, one of his favorite authors, whom he had even visited. The French writer had supposedly refused to see visitors, but had naturally made an exception for Rudolf. "In dreams one can think of the last writer, with whom the small mystery of written expression disappears when he dies, without anyone noticing. To paint the situation a bit more fantastically, we can think of him as Rimbaud, a Rimbaud reaching even further into the mystical, a poet who feels inside himself his form of expression becoming mute and knows it will die with him. Finally, we can assume that this end—in one way or the other—will be irrevocable as an end, in the world and in the cycle of cultures. And what would follow? Surely, a profound silence. This is what we say out of courtesy when any writer disappears from the earth: a voice has been silenced, a way of thinking is gone. What a silence would have to follow if there were no longer anyone who understood that special way of talking represented by the whole body of the famous works of world literature."

The second motto was from Cesare Pavese:

> Death has a look for everyone.
> Death will come and will have your eyes.
> It will be like renouncing a vice,
> like seeing a dead face
> reappear in the mirror,
> like listening to a lip that's shut.
> We'll go down into the maelstrom mute.

My hands were shaking. Rudolf, who had visited me in dreams almost every night to discuss all sorts of details that

I could not remember in the morning, was suddenly so close that I involuntarily looked around. A way of thinking is gone. I would have to summon all my strength to keep from falling apart.

Next page. First chapter, 1963, "Shame," written in red, and underneath, with a fine black felt pen (probably a Stabilo; he'd been very fond of them), the column:

> Yellow notebook, 1963, pp. 20–24. Box 16.
> Old University, pp. 14–15, 19, 21, 17–90, 212 [marked]. Box 19.
> Dossier M: Letter (3).
> Yellow notebook, 1963, pp. 1–18. Box 16.
> Green notebook (2), 1989. Box 36.
> Correspondence E, (17), (18), (19), with responses. Box 12.
> Dossier E1: (4), (7), (9).
> Yellow notebook, 1963, p. 19 [marked], pp. 37–56. Box 16.
> Emrich seminar: (3), (4). Box 19.
> Dossier R: (1) with deletions!
> Dossier Eva: (3), (4), (7).
> Dossier M: Letter 4 [marked].
> Old University, Document 5, Box 19.
> Black notebook, 1966, pp. 12–31. Box 17.

And on and on, page after page.

There was no doubt that this painstaking listing, which he had drawn up for all twenty chapters, was the framework of the novel that now lay before me, divided up into boxes, waiting to be pulled together, and which, probably, I had inadvertently destroyed. I had always been awed by Rudolf's memory, which could retain everything—every triviality, every malicious remark, but especially every detail of the books he had read. Whenever and wherever a lie was told, he immediately had the great lie-chapters of world literature ready to hand: every conceivable father-son, mother-child example of the lie would come to mind as soon as he needed them. He could have whipped together an anthology on any subject—jealousy, brothels—in an hour, from memory. Who or what does that hat remind you of, or this dog, or that fat guy over there? He would ask me these questions on our walks, when he was in good spirits, and would immediately provide examples out of world literature—from Kierkegaard, Hawthorne, or Faulkner, from Marx or Adorno. When he was in a bad mood, though, he would laugh bitterly whenever I had, as usual, forgotten something that belonged in "our book of memories," as he put it. He liked to say that we all have memory books of our own, into which we enter the most important occurrences of our life, and that we should always be memorizing; we mustn't forget a single detail. But just as important, he would add, are the memory books we keep and share with others, which consist in part of ordinary things that even after ten years can revive immediate mutual understanding—things such as puns, silly jokes, common experiences, but also matters of substance. What he meant by "substance" was never clear to me, but how sacred this substance was became apparent the minute it was touched on by anyone outside our circle and had to be defended. Part of it consisted, naturally, of a small group of books that had played a role in our story: woe to anyone who sullied these works in our presence! Moreover, Rudolf could become downright vicious if I were to remark casually that, on rereading it, I no longer cared so much for one of our sacred books—for instance, Hoffmann's fairy tale *The Golden Pot,* which he once gave me in a very early edition that had been presented to him by the East German historian Jürgen Kuczynski. (During the time of the student revolts, Rudolf had had an extensive correspondence with Kuczynski, who, as I had just seen, was to play a big role in the eighth chapter of his novel.) "You can make a motion," Rudolf had written by return mail. "I can tell you now, though, that the motion will be rejected: *The Golden Pot* is staying in our kitchen."

Now, I asked myself, who is supposed to take this final memory book, this gigantic collage, made up of postcards and train tickets, hotel and restaurant checks, and turn it into a readable novel?

After I had read the last twenty pages, including the "Farewell" (which was to consist almost completely of our five dossiers and was supposed to conclude with a poem dedicated to me), I found a letter from Rudolf, addressed to me, dated two days before his death.

My dear friend,

I assume that you are reading these lines in my study, drinking a bottle of Barolo, which you have found in the pantry. Elsa (who has cancer, incidentally, something I was not allowed to tell anyone) will have called you and asked you to go through my unpublished papers, and, knowing you as I do, I am sure you complied with her request immediately. Don't bother yourself with the papers in my offices at the institute or at the university; all of that is the worthless stuff that everybody leaves behind, at least everyone who ever spent a lifetime working in an office. The university president, whom you have probably met by now, might have an interest in confiscating all that, because he (quite rightly) will assume that it includes documents on a few scandals that I uncovered. The only things that matter are the gray boxes. Watch out, by the way, for Marta, who has an unpleasant proclivity for cultivated older gentlemen, which not even my foul moods could completely discourage. I have written the number of each box on its lid—there must be sixty-four of them. If even one is missing, it will be catastrophic for my book—in such an event you will have to put the squeeze on Marta.

Making the complete compilation should not present any difficulties for you if you follow my directions precisely. For me, a task of this kind is just too repulsive. I neither could, nor would I wade once more through the swamp of my life, having slogged through it in my mind so many times. This novel has turned into a sensational bildungsroman, as we literary men say. By the way, you might need to add or delete a word at some of the junctures in the work, although I think I have noted down everything in the documents myself. But you never know. The hard cuts are intentional, of course. Please destroy any material that is left over. Everything that does not go into the book goes into the wastebasket. Please follow these instructions, and don't try playing the part of Dr. Brod.

I have been entirely sincere in composing this final work; it will not win me any favor with the critics, although out of posthumous vanity I still hope for that. But it's of no consequence. As far as I know, this book will be the most accurate description extant of the sixty years of German postwar history; except for those few stories still in print, there is no other history of the period worth speaking of. And I believe it will show that there are good reasons to respect our country—its arrogance and mediocrity notwithstanding.

You may and must decide whether the book should be published or not. If it is, it must be published only in this form. Of course you have the right to change names, or replace them with initials.

If you wish, you can publish the book under your own name, I have no problem with that. The copyright on words I find offensive anyway. But you must make sure, in any event, that the honorarium is divided equally among Elsa, Eva, Marta, and you, the unwilling co-authors of this collective work.

Should you decide against publication, which is totally up to you, I ask you to destroy the blue folio with the table of contents, and, of course, this letter along with it. I should not like to see you go down in history as either a forger or a suppressor of literary work.

The moment has come when nothing more remains to be said. Say goodbye to Caesar for me, whom I hope you have found still alive—he is an old fellow, plagued with illnesses—and to the other animals. I will remain in touch with Elsa, Eva, and Marta by other means.

I remember clearly the day I moved in with you and our friendship began, with Kafka as our third mate. Take good care of Eva. The stuff she writes is *unreadable, but you don't really have to read it.*

Thank you for everything, and forgive the circumstances of my departure!

From the deathbed of literature, I bid you farewell.

Your Rudolf

I sat looking at this letter for a long while, numb. Outside, dawn was slowly breaking, the edges of the clouds brightening. I strode one more time through all the rooms in the apartment, touching objects, saying farewell. I took the dossiers and the folio with the table of contents and added them to the other documents in my overnight bag. As I left the building, it was six o'clock. Unless it was running late, the train would leave the Turin station in thirty-two minutes.